SATURN SPLIT

A NOVEL
BY
ALAN GLAZEN

"If there's no lion in the mountains, the monkey will be king."
–Confuscious

 Chicago Spectrum Press
1571 Sherman, Annex C
Evanston, IL 60201

All author's income from the first edition will be donated to
Providence House, the crisis nursery, in Cleveland, Ohio

ISBN: 1-886094-02-0

Manufactured in the United States of America

Editor: Kathy Kelly
Typesetting: Luanne Kirwan
Design: Sue Monahan
Cover Graphics: Brian Willse

Prologue

The great walled city is quiet with tension as all of the three major religions simultaneously celebrate that each is right and the other two are, therefore, wrong.

Maybe tonight.

You, on the other hand, are merely driving between your new job and your old house, thanking your lucky stars that Toledo is on the way. Toledo is your oasis. The town appears a bit tense in its non-activity, a lot of potential lurking in every bar and bowling alley. Which to choose? Where to find comfort? Nothing going on but a few ordinary fellows strolling out the double door up ahead, a bar. A working class bar where everyone loves the Marlboro Man.

Everyone anticipates it. It has to happen some time.

No offense to the Jews, but Jerusalem is in a state of permanent limbo since they decided to embrace the ancient belief that the Messiah won't fly over gravesites. Oh, yes, and that he must come from the East. The limbo, they'd say, was caused by the Arabs who conveniently surrounded the East entrance to the city with burial grounds. Even the Messiah would be confused by this sneaky little trick. He'll have to make his entrance somewhere else. Another doorway. It could be anywhere.

One thing everyone shares is a certainty that he's coming.

This created a great quandary among the members of the Jewish faith. No one competes with the Jews when it comes to symbolizing something they believe in. Passover dinner, for example, where a place is set for the Messiah so he'll feel right at home no matter which doorway he enters. The big question is "How will we know him when we see him? How will we know he arrived?"

No problem for this imaginative people. They simply determined that there would always be 36 people living who, unbeknownst to them, would somehow know when the Messiah arrives. And they'd be individually drawn to him like ants to a honey pot.

Well, now there you have it. A spiritual early warning system with human sirens. You can imagine a piercing shriek going off alerting us to Messiah arrival. If it could only be in our lifetimes. Wouldn't you hate to miss it by just a few days?

The Jews named this special bunch "The Lamed Vav," which means "The 36." When Jews name a thing, they keep in mind how it will sound if it ends up being a major motion picture. You never know.

Lo and behold! You just happen to be on that surreptitious route, minding your own business, looking for a sign that says they'll understand you here.

Chapter One

You are, after all, completely common. But you push the twin doors open and, in your little mind, cartoony puffs of smoke pop out of your ears as everyone drops to the ground at the mere sight of you. June does that to people, and apparently has an even greater effect on your imagination.

No one's exactly swooning at your presence, but you have entered with a certain sense of nobility and two of the three sets of eyes glance toward you, not bad for a fellow who has always been pretty easy to ignore. Why, you don't know. Maybe it's your size. You're actually at your biggest, 172 pounds, 5 foot 9, give or take a half inch. Mostly take. Still have that curly hair that you hated when you were a kid.

You went through a short period of time when everyone took note of your hair, but even then, no one took note of you. But today you are feeling a bit more confident than usual. You carry a certain pride today. This morning you clipped your nose hairs with that electric gizmo that came for free with your shaver. Funny that for the first 40 years of your life, it never occured to you that your nose hairs required attention. Heaven knows what revelations life has in store for you.

Your arrival is unfortunately marred when the artificial fleece hanging from the back hem of your brown leather jacket gets caught in the dilapidated metal screen. No eyes roll but you're sure the eye muscles are contracting.

That's how much you believe in your own presence.

Your head turns toward the bar and you can tell that your elbows are going to feel comforted by the well-worn counter. There's a fellow sitting there alone who wouldn't look inappropriate wearing a beanie with a twirly propeller whirling away even when the air is still.

He seems to be turning toward you. There must be someone walking in behind you. You don't expect to be greeted in a place where no one knows you. This is a very nice moment if the greeting is intended for you, but it could be very embarrassing if it's not. You'd be very happy leaving.

But you're here so that's where you ought to be. You're a passive guy, and fate is fate. All you want is to be authentic to yourself. To believe in yourself not so much for your potential but just for coming close to your own definition.

But you can't know yourself entirely, so you need a bit of latitude in your definition of what it takes to believe in something. You're willing to look the other way from time to time in exchange for the comfort of knowing you have a belief.

To accept what you are is your greatest source of pride. You amounted to very little. You don't intimidate anyone. Your English literature degree has not gotten you far.

All those years of struggling to memorize the sonnets of Shakespeare, battles of the Civil War and the atomic weights of the elements did not pay off. No one could conjugate like you but this talent is rarely requested outside of your little editing nook at the cook book place.

Your keen ability to sum things up quickly, to deduce a weakness or inclination in a perfect stranger, your fundamental grasp of human nature – all of these attributes somehow never united within you. Your strengths after all these years have remained perfect strangers.

All of this comfortably set aside, it is not a mistake for people to sum you up by how you look.

But, how you look makes you fit in.

Big deal. How startling an achievement is this in Toledo, Ohio, home of the Mud Hens. No one seems to be sure of what sport they play.

And here he comes, Mr. Bubbly Personality. "Hey, there, welcome to Danny's, how're ya doing?" The guy's foremost feature is his girth.

He walks you to the stool as if you'd been walking and talking about exciting topics for hours.

Across the room, a pair of little eagle eyes peer over the torn Oriental divider which separates the bar area from a foodless kitchen. Hunger feels like an appropriate theme for the place.

You take a deep breath and note that the welcoming committee is a cab driver. The back of his pants are almost too perfectly indented with wooden beads. You can imagine him at night ironing his pants over them, just to look perfectly genuine. But you smile as two guys talk about nothing.

You buy a beer and the chubby cabby returns to his sparkling cocktail catching a murky redness from the naugahyde stool beside it. The seat is slit just a little near the center. The stuffing is visible but it's not coming out, so you can understand why it hasn't been re-covered.

You came in because it's hot outside. The Maumee river looks sweaty. The air is wet. The entire environment has conspired to get you here.

Somehow, you feel that there are new possibilities surrounding you. How could this fake pine paneled lounge with one man stumbling for the words to express hello, the other altogether too alert to your arrival, stir you in the slightest way?

A certain tension mounts.

Never been to Toledo. Never been in Danny's Talk of the Town. Never seen a horse's head mounted on the wall of a bar.

Forgetting all of these complications, there is the simple truth that you'll be back here many times. Your company's been moved from Geneva on the

Lake to a fake log cabin building just off I-90 near the Michigan border. Danny's is on the way.

The cabby's Toledo Mud Hens sweat band is dry despite the heat.

"Kind of nice to know they still have hacks in the big city. How's business?" you ask the friendly generous cheeks with the little rubbery lips that look like where you inflate him. He's sucking on a celery stalk sticking out of his glass. The celery seems to do a good job of sealing him up.

His lips only part enough for the words to eke out, and they open before the words arrive. You expect them to be out of synch with his mouth movements.

You glance toward the Oriental divider and see that the beady eyes are contained in a beady head attached to a very short but stout body.

"It ain't so good, but I'm getting some other things started. How about you?" he asks. He's a good conversation starter

Friendly place, this Danny's Talk of the Town. Twenty seats around the oval brown bar, top brands scattered here and there to make it look like that's all they carry. The previously noted horse's head coming out the wall. Not a deer or an antelope. It's wearing a baseball cap embroidered with the word POPE.

Half a dozen television sets of various vintages, none of this epoch, play the same thing, a cowboy movie that for the last 15 minutes has been inter-rupted by a pitch for impregnable vinyl windows. You know the commercial is in color, but at Danny's Talk of the Town, even the color TV's play every-thing in fuzzy black and white.

"And if you call right now, you'll receive this full color brochure," the kooky little blond girl promises. Imagine, full color. Others might not understand, but you appreciate this promise. Full color versus something less colorful, something less convincing. Something cheap and quick that no one had real confidence in.

Inching up over the divider is the bald, rotund head of Danny DeMarco. His eyes are like friendly little leeches, attaching themselves to you, but not actually taking anything in.

You can tell by his eyes that running this place is just an in-between thing, that something else is oc-curring. His head turns to keep the pupils centered as he scans the room like a motorized burglar cam-era.

"Everything okay over there? Can I bring you some fresh popcorn?" he catches your eye and you feel exhaustion setting in.

"Yeah, sure, is there a charge?" you ask because even though you have about $32 with you, it's im-portant that in these early stages, no one can take you for a chump.

"On the house, and the butter's real," Danny answers proudly as he fills a bowl and spritzes hot, very yellow butter over it.

"My work's steady," you answer the cab driver who seems to find your response very enlightening.

"Now you see, that's an interesting option. What do you mean, steady, exactly?" he turns to you and rests his chin on his hand.

Danny in his crisply washed and pressed white apron approaches with the popcorn. You can see that the apron is rolled about an inch thick at the waist to make up for it being made for a regular sized person, and Danny being only about five foot two.

"Would the two of you care for another drink?" he asks, but he isn't asking the two of you or just the cabby. He's asking you.

"Uh, yeah, well, sure, another beer please."

"And for your friend?" he's still looking at you.

You feel set-up, but what the hell, a beer with a stranger, why not be a sport? "Well, why not?" you pat the cab driver's back. A beer with a new friend, it's kind of tribal and expansive.

"What'll you have? By the way, I'm Al," you offer your hand and he shakes it very firmly. He's very happy to meet you.

The cab driver asks for a glass of champagne.

"Sure, coming right up," Danny is happy too.

"Champagne, very nice," you say.

"I taught myself to like it," he apologizes.

"Try a drop of Chambord and it gets a little sweet and fruity," you advise him.

So you continue enjoying the conversation and you're actually surprised to see how good it feels. As he warms up, the guy gets good at keeping things going, and you don't feel under the normal pressure to invent things to talk about.

You're not even upset that the bill for the two drinks comes to $11.80, because after all, a place this nice and hospitable that draws such a good hearted crowd is worth a small premium.

On your way out you turn to wave good-bye to the cabby and it occurs to you that he never actually gave you his name. How silly of you. Anyway, you say "Good talking to you," and he answers "Zeke." And your evening ends on the upbeat note that someone liked you enough to reveal his name. This is the perfect time to be gone, and out you go to the beckoning emptiness of your remaining day.

"Now, Zeke, we need to learn from this here," Danny leans over the cab driver's shoulder. Danny's shortness has a certain tightly bound tallness about it.

"I thought I was doing good. I liked the guy." The cabby tries to cut the conversation short.

"He's our kind of fellow," Danny replies. "I couldn't

keep him much longer without him wondering, and anyway he's new and I'll bet he'll be back before you know it." Zeke explains.

"But he was here. You didn't optimize the immediate. There's got to be a maximized return, you know what I mean?" he lectures.

"Next time, I'll do better, I promise. You're right," Zeke hopes to conclude.

"Okay, I know you understand. Okay?" he pats him on the cheek.

"Yeah, yeah."

Danny DeMarco. They used to call him Dandy.
He moved out of his neighborhood on the West Side
and got all new friends before he finally escaped
that embarrassment. He'd have changed families
too, except there was no need to. The only one still
alive was his great aunt Hanna, and she had emphysema so bad she couldn't call him anything.

Frannie, on the other hand, called him lots of
things.

"Danny, you're a scumbag!" Fran interrupts Danny's thought process, him laying on her lacy bed
watching World Wide Wrestling on her little black
and white television set.

"A scumbag," he parrots her.

"Danny, you're just a big finagler. You told me we
would see a show tonight!" she whines but not in a
nagging way.

He chews on the sides of his tongue and emits a
brief chortle followed by, "what do you mean?"

"A show! Going out for a change!" she bops his
nose with hers.

"This is a show. We stayed in. You're one and one.
Settle for it," he draws a circle on her forehead with
the tip of his tongue.

"Yuck," she sighs.

She goes back to her favorite magazine, "WORLD
GALAXY" and flips immediately past the special
"X-Rays of Famous Stars" feature to find out what

her own star has in store for her:

"Your personal growth period continues, so don't be surprised if you develop urges to beat yourself up. Be proud that you can take it. Saturn is in your second house. Think of it as that nun who whacks your knuckles for impure thoughts. If you're a little hyper these days, it's that nasty taskmaker planet's fault. Just keep listening and doing what you're told for just a bit longer and it will all pay off someday soon."

"Guess what?" Frannie says to Danny.

"Spare me," he answers.

"Saturn's in my second house now," she says.

"That's very nice. I hope that Saturn is comfy there."

"Saturn has been in my horoscope as long as I can remember. It's a plague. I don't know how much more I can take of it!" she says with real concern. "Pluto was one thing. Saturn is unbearable, like a curse," she adds. "It always seems to be one or another."

"Yes, they are quite pesky planets," he smirks, not realizing that Saturn is the weight of the universe on her shoulders.

Danny turns to the TV just as Gorilla Manson is trying to implant his gigantic black wrestling boot in the mouth of the mangy-haired Hispanic opponent who has been mangled since he entered the ring.

She gets up and sprays her bosom with cologne, right through her frilly little doily pajamas. She seems completely comfortable with their translucency, rendering the designer's intentions oddly asexual. Her comfort with her body has contributed to Danny's lack of sexual interest in her, just his luck he often mourns.

"Look who's a finagler!" he grabs the bottle and reads the label.

"Vertigo," he reads.

"Now if I get a stiffy when I smell this on you, does this mean I get you?"

She blows air in her cheeks and smirks at him.

"It's looks for look's sake," she laughs.

"Yeah, well I only order French fries for the catsup."

This is why she loves him. This state of total confusion is very liberating to her. Without a chance of understanding anything, she doesn't have to try. She doesn't have to feel bad because she's confused. Being confused is fun.

The Hispanic wrestler spits out the boot and drives his fist in to Gorilla's midsection. Gorilla responds with an elbow across the forehead, which the commentator refers to as a scientific hold.

"Or do you just like to shake it?" she whispers devilishly.

**Chapter
Three**

The American Council of Bishops is a happy place today. Bishop Hutt's bleached pine floor with that subtle whitewash finish is gleaming with the reflection from his billowy red velour robe.

He grasps the wafer thin silver remote controller, aims it at the Bang & Olufson CD player with the transparent acrylic cover.

Some Windham Hill collection plays a repulsively melodious spiritual ditty as Bishop Hutt dismisses the handful of reporters. The big news is in. The Vatican has announced that the downward cycle of church contributions has ended.

Public relations, of course, was Bishop Hutt's background, which he was proud to have learned played a strong part in the council having appointed him to this key role. In fact, had his recent predecessor applied proper accounting and public relation skills to this matter, he would have made a similar announcement years ago.

Basically, the strategy was based on one simple revelation: Who gives money to a lost cause? Look successful, be successful. And, what the heck, self-fulfilling or not, prophecies are right at home here in the Vatican.

He had been so bubbly and eloquent, so charming for a man of the cloth to get such a giggle out of playing with numbers.

"In fact, truth to speak, it's a complete aberration

that caused us to think there ever was a downward trend! We were doing just fine, all along, thank you!" he lied so delightfully.

The ACB is a much more optimistic place even now, as he removes his custom fit "Ear," the molded plastic little speaker that lets him hear a recording of his speech so he can mimic it as he actually performs it.

He will be well-regarded for this news.

Chapter Four

Weeks later, you've been to Danny's every few days. You're driving back home and here you are again. Suddenly you've become a Danny's customer, settling in, feeling accustomed.

It's not that you're the bar type. You just need a break. You've been writing and rewriting that Asparagus book. You keep trying out the steamed with pesto and it never tastes crisp enough. Inconsistencies galore. Some measurements 24 ounces, other times a pound and a half. It's amazing how much latitude you can give in human situations, and how precise you demand the small measurements to be.

Of course, Zeke is here. You've caught on to his thing. Danny probably thinks it is entirely reasonable to have someone selling drinks like a saleswoman working the cosmetics counter. But in this context, it's so completely silly, you never let on that you're aware of it. And you never ask where he parks his taxi.

"Zeke, I think this one should be on you, what do you say?" you tease him, knowing that he'll get killed if he causes the bar to cough up money on you. At least he ought to dance or something.

You can imagine him shaking it up for tips.

You've also been noticing the meek looking fellow around 55, with thinning but long and uncombed light red hair. He hasn't shaved for several days but his facial hair just doesn't look like it could grow in to a beard. It's more like stubble in pieces, like the lead in a mechanical pencil, breaking away so another whole piece can instantly push through.

You can see some of the pieces on his yellow, brushed cotton shirt that's haphazardly tucked in to his wool green, red and purple plaid pants.

You can hear him talking to Danny, and the nice thing about this place is that it seems perfectly fine to pick a chair close enough so you can overhear.

You're all in it together.

"Everything I know I learned from two sources and neither of them were school," Danny explains to the gangly man.

"And those were?" asks Father Terry Mulroy whose tender but roughed up face and red-rivered nose belies his argument that his pulpit was stolen out from under him. His gentle eyes somehow explain why he won't talk any further about it.

"Wrestling and religion," Danny points to the television set hanging from its black metal hospital mounting over the bar. A beer-bellied fellow in black shorts and cheap tennis shoes is getting spun in the air by a human bumble bee with warpaint and electrifying tights.

"Wrestling and religion, a lovely alliance," the gravely voice responds, offering to hear more, but certainly not demanding it.

"What you see is real because it's happening,"

Danny explains. "Whether or not it's even the least bit honest is irrelevant. What counts is what you see and how you feel while you're involved with it. The primary goal is to shut your senses down and just go with it."

"Meaning?"

"Meaning you know that wrestling is fake but you suspend your disbelief in exchange for the entertainment and the drama."

"And religion?"

"Same thing. You get a nice, tidy little package that explains it all. You're so excited to have found a set of truths that fit together, your euphoria masks your confusion," Danny explains like an excited school teacher, and even Father Mulroy, having heard this all before, is often astounded at Danny's intellect.

"It's all sitting there nice and pretty ready to be capitalized on," Danny concludes, and Father Mulroy is reminded that Danny's intellect is unfortunately partnered with Danny's greed and lust.

"Well, Danny, surely you have an interest in religion that is bigger than profitability!" Father Mulroy gently suggests.

"Of course, there is the big question which would be nice to have answered," Danny admits.

"The big question being?"

"Does life count enough that it matters whether

our feelings are stimulated by real or phony experiences?" Danny answers with a conclusive wave of his hands as he turns his head, notices you are listening, and waits for you to nod your head in agreement too.

"Does it matter whether what you believe in is real or not? That's the issue, and that, Father Terry, is what it's all about."

You dare to join the conversation.

"I've never heard anyone talk about religion and belief in terms of profitability. How do those relate?" you ask.

Father Mulroy seems to find your question appropriate. Danny, on the other hand, rolls his eyes and practically swoons at your stupidity.

"You ever been to the Vatican?" he challenges you.

'Not lately," you answer.

"It's a money machine. It's Las Vegas east. Money. Gold. Art. Religion is just the conveyor belt to carry it all in and out," Danny rattles.

"That's a bit insulting, wouldn't you say?" Father Mulroy interrupts.

"Sure, to those who are the exception. I don't have time for the exception here. The big picture is cash. They should have it hanging on the walls. They should make stained glass montages of various currencies." Danny drives on.

"Jesus did not appear to be motivated by cash," you offer.

"I can't answer for him. But I know one thing. Religion was invented to stop us from killing each other, pure and simple, so life could go on for those who profit from it," Danny answers, his eyes turning toward Zeke who doesn't want anything to do with this and is totally absorbed by his Pink Lady.

"So you feel that none of what we believe is true?" Father Mulroy tries to put closure on the conversation.

"If none of it was true, we'd have made it up anyway. It is, in all fairness, the perfect story," he concludes.

"The Bible?" you ask.

"A work of absolute genius," Danny answers proudly, as if he wrote it.

"The bottom line is still whether you believe or you don't," suggests the Father.

"It all works out the same whether you believe it or not. How sane can we be having imminent death hanging over our heads every moment of every day?" Danny smiles.

"The long and short of it, to me, is you've got to believe in something to get through it," you add.

"My friend, the long and short of it is, as long as people believe, who gets the merchandising rights?" Danny pounds his fist on the shaky counter.

"Let me just say this –" mutters the Father cling-ing to his last shreds of loyalty to a church which has rejected him.

"You could be right but it wouldn't matter. Faith and truth are not separate ideas. Faith is more true than truth. We believe our hearts more than we be-lieve our eyes and ears, which is why when the Pope arrives in a city, not a soul questions his position. No one asks if this man is holy."

"They picked him because he looks and acts holy!!!" Danny blurts.

"You're suggesting the Pope could be just any-body?" you assert.

"Jesus could be anybody!!" Danny screeches.

"Isn't that what Jesus was all about in the first place?" Mulroy responds solemnly, but with a smile.

Zeke strolls over to the Father's little round table as Danny's attention is diverted by a new customer, a young woman in blue jeans and a man's freshly pressed white shirt. Zeke notices you and says "Hey Al, I'm glad to see you. Stick around and we'll lift a few, you know," and he smiles as he approaches the Father.

"How ya doing, Father? You and I should lift a few too." Zeke's entire face greets the Father in his best friendly manner.

"I've already lifted my share, thank you."

"Well, I've always wanted to have a chance to talk

to someone in your position. Can I ask how you happened to become a priest?" Zeke asks as he pulls up a chair and looks like a real good listener.

"Well, if you're interested, I was driven by the same thing that moves most people."

"How's that?" Zeke helps him continue.

"Confusion! I needed a chance to think and have my basic needs provided for so I might come up with an answer, an idea that I could share with others." It was a nice answer.

"What kind of ideas have you come up with?" asks Zeke as Danny returns his attention to the table looking exasperated that Zeke is working the Father.

"Off limits Zeke," he says straight out.

Zeke's forehead forms a question mark. Father Mulroy's adds an exclamation.

"I mean I was in the middle of a discussion, would you mind, Zeke?" Danny attempts to be polite.

"Not at all, Danny, good to meet you Father," and he walks away to his station at the bar, awaiting another simple soul with another need for conversation.

As most people categorize others by their personality types, Danny thinks of people as wallet-types. There are eelskins, the kind that have more flash on the outside than on the inside. And there are cowhides, with bigger credit limits than paychecks. And there is the Velcro set, wilderness types who love to say they don't mind mosquitoes, yeah sure.

Father Mulroy is an exception. He has no wallet. However one defines failure, he is one, except that he has a very kind if quirky heart. Most people with little to give appear to be generous. Danny is more attracted to failure than he is to success. He has always hated success stories, far preferring riches to rags, the demise of a billionaire, always a delight.

"I have no curiosity about the rich," he'd often say.

"It's easy to understand their motives, how they achieve them, how they get by," he would continue.

"But the poor, the failures, the seedy, the rubble, they are the mysteries. Their happiness is the biggest mystery of all," and that's why he would sacrifice the extra drink income from the Father in exchange for some insight.

"That's why I like you," Danny delivers a sharp body blow which goes by unnoticed by the Father.

"Jesus died for my sins," Father Mulroy soothes him.

"If Jesus died for your sins, then what are you expecting from him when he returns? What's he coming back for?" asks Danny as Zeke begins his approach to the young woman at the bar. He goes very slowly on the woman to be sure he is giving off no sexual intentions. He is very careful to come across as one of those rare guys who really just wants to hear what a woman has on her mind. The woman would have to suggest anything more than that.

"I'm expecting cataclysm, of course," Mulroy says after thinking for a second. "Especially if he ever linked up with you," he jokes.

"Everything is fine, as I have reported!" the stout Bishop Hutt speaks reassuringly into the mouthpiece as he fondles the turbomouse attached to his OptiQuad 210 laptop.

"My dear Bishop, I understand the value of being a settling influence, but what about your faith?" asks the calm feminine man speaking over the tense long distance line connecting his sparse little office in Vatican City to Bishop Hutt's slick, contemporary office suite in Washington.

"I have a great deal of faith. We have a great leader, a great humanitarian, a great spirit to guide us," says Hutt, very deliberately, careful to avoid sounding condescending in his response.

"I'm talking about your faith in the numbers," the little voice interrupts.

"What are you asking me?" Bishop Hutt asks coyly.

"Your joyous announcement about our collections has been very reassuring. Between you and me and the lamp post, what is the truth?"

"The truth is that we're a sick puppy," the Bishop says forthrightly.

"I see," the meek voice responds.

"We need new sources of revenue."

"I see," the voice repeats.

"The Jews, they get membership dues; the Witnesses sell books and magazines, the Greeks, they sell Holy Sardines in Jerusalem. We're late starters," explains Bishop Hutt.

"And we?" asks the voice.

"We need our own thing."

"We knighted Kurt Waldheim," his voice beams.

"Point made. We need something new," the Bishop moans.

After exchanging some pleasant little convivialities, the colleagues in holiness say good-bye, Bishop Hutt promising to explore the possibilities. The other man can't understand why the Church must deal in things like electric bills and exterminating contracts. It just seems so unworthy!

Chapter Six

Each visit to Danny's would feel like a single frame excerpted from a very talky kind of movie. The same characters, punctuated from time to time by a few strangers who'd never been there before, who'd probably be back, all hoping to become regulars.

You would look forward to going there even though nothing whatsoever ever came of it. A little taste of this or that conversation, Danny responding to all conversations the same way. Whatever you believe in is simply something which has fooled you, and he, of course, sees through it all.

You sit in your editor's nook at the recipe place and visualize yourself pounding beers at Danny's, knowing full well that there really isn't enough significance in the beer or the conversation to justify anything more than sipping.

But the place is filled with promise. Somehow you just know that some day, all the crazy little pieces of sanity will unite and form one adult idea that some goofy person, probably Danny, will actually run with.

Here you are sitting at your desk, pounding away on the typewriter. Whoever wrote the original draft did not understand how words could create pastures of greenery, beds of rainbow colors. Some people delight in being decidedly unflowery.

You give them petals.

This is what you do. You're a romantic and a eunuch. You are unattached to even your own words, yet there's still the chance that someday, you'll combine your special observation skills with your editor's sense of flow and style.

There was a time in high school when you were quite the poet, writing under a fake name so no one could tease you for the beauty of your words.

If only Laura Weller had not made fun of your kissing ability that night behind Park High School. If only she had not ended up back there the next night with your best friend, Scott.

That's when your words became barbed and angry. "The earth is starving and I'm being swallowed." "Shotguns for everyone and television sets." Lyrics to mean-spirited songs that would have depressed everyone by both their nature and their truth.

You were a secret Romeo to scores of girls whose popularity frightened you out of revealing your passions with your name attached. You once sent an anonymous Valentine telegram to a 13 year-old girl telling her you worship her every word. The next day at school, she and her friends almost knocked you over as they walked down the school hallway laughing at your words.

From that time on, you were a "behind-the-scenes" type man.

Life is easier now. Your simple side won. You look like no bother to anyone. This lets you get closer than most would otherwise tolerate if you were a man of presence. It's your key to other people's private space. Eavesdropping is your favorite hobby. Zeke has become your microphone.

You get ideas and revelations you never share because you must protect your sources. They reveal your inadequacy as a participant in friendships.

And, of course you have become a very forgiving man. How else could you deal with yourself?

It's hard not to be a regular at Talk of the Town. The criteria are very simple. Come in from time to time. Buy something. Leave soon. You'll always be welcomed back.

But you can't imagine ending up sharing dinner with someone you met here, being invited to meet the wife and kids.

You are definitely a regular like Zeke the cabby, pretty much there all the time and never a cab in sight. He cuts a figure not unlike your own, hopefully just a bit more ordinary looking, but you admit to yourself that aside from your full head of curly hair at 41, there's nothing all too memorable about you.

You used to weigh 165 and now you've grown to 172. It's all in your belly. You're pretty sure you'd sacrifice your handsome legs for a beefier pair if your belly would tone down a bit and make you look stocky rather than lazy.

There's always Danny, constantly studying, dissecting. You can close your eyes and picture full bodies walking in, skeletons walking out. It's a very draining place considering how little it asks of you. Just sit down and fit in.

And you can't help but notice that the decor evolves, every now and then a new sweatshirt hanging like a trophy, a baseball cap sitting obscenely on the horse's head.

This time the hat reads "Pope On Tour," undoubtedly another one of those nasty, noisy heavy metal groups. The last group you really went for was The Four Seasons. You saw them seven times in seven years, every time at the same place, Adelbert Gymnasium in Cleveland, Ohio, an hour and a half away. But in those days, a group always sounded better live than on the record.

You also can't help but notice that whenever Danny's black spotted eyes weren't anywhere to be found, you'd hear this clackity clackity sound, like a computer printer, except there'd be no computer printer at Talk of the Town. What for? A spreadsheet with one column? A story with one paragraph?

One day when Danny was pre-occupied with Father Mulroy, you took a look behind the screen and saw this alien machine, a metal stalk emanating from a computer-like contraption. And you saw some blank baseball caps and T-Shirts strewn around. What an odd side-business for a bar, you thought, humored at the vision of this little pip of a man laboring in secrecy over a covert computer embroidery business.

Talk of the Town was more relaxed than, say, a titty bar with table dancers, although the intimacy was a bit similar in its sense of having been fabricated and well-used.

Maybe it was more like the vestibule outside the main hall at Church where the minister welcomes you and wishes you well right before the President of Church Council glares at you for having once again forgotten to pay your pledge money.

Does God really know, you always wonder? Is church the toll-gate to heaven?

"It'd make your prayers rise a lot higher, Al. It'd make them a lot easier for you-know-who to hear!" the President would say.

The customers at Talk of the Town don't have to deal with that kind of pressure. They aren't there to see any private parts or to ask any private questions. Everyone always seems to be real accustomed to sitting at a bar and looking like they've been there before.

You, for one, could only do this with practice, because you were still honest enough to recognize that the only reason you're alone is because you don't really have any actual friends.

But you're open to the possibility, as long as it doesn't involve any long dull stories that result in resentment toward you for having passively stuck your nose in someone else's affairs.

You've noticed that your hair really does set you apart. It's the only hair at Danny's that doesn't look like it was fed a poor diet as a child. Most of the others' remaining hairs look stringy. Too much luncheon meat with odd splotches of mysterious organs stranded in the coagulation.

But aside from simple grooming distinctions, everyone here is pretty much the same in their loneliness and their act of gathering together in their loneliness to make it look like something else.

You turn to the right and see a 20 year old who is too young to be part of this scene. His face appears to be grieving. He's considering giving up already instead of enrolling in college, sitting under a tree studying with some freckle-faced girl, secretly working her toward some drunken night when she'll cave in.

Here at Danny's no such possibilities exist. There are no significant common interests at this point. You're pretty much left with the weather and the Mud Hens, and these conversations tend to be similar and short.

"You like rock n roll?" you ask the young fellow kindly as you lift your beer to his good health.

"Course I do," he tips his beer in your direction without smiling. He appears to be fearful as if he was here just to check his status against the lowest denominator.

Being too friendly is like seeming too hungry. Any kind of excess seems desperate. Looking lonely does not have to seem desperate if you look comfortable with it. That's why so many lonely people are so unusually egotistical. They've conditioned themselves to believe that their solitude is by choice.

"I'd like to understand the attraction of this music. What do you like best about it?" you continue as he listens without warming up a degree.

There is no music playing, of course, because the screens are filled with the Three Stooges, and for a moment you recall how proud you once were of your ability to snap your fingers like Mo.

Danny looks at you with pleasant curiosity. He seems to like that you're making an effort to meet someone new and make him feel at home.

"You mean what group?" your new friend mutters, so easily tormented, yet, it was his decision to come here! He could have gone to the convenience store for a beer.

"Yeah. Like, uh –" and you can't think of a single music group but you notice the rock n roll baseball cap on the horse and figure he'd relate to whoever it is commemorating. "Like Pope or whatever," you toss out lightly.

"Who is Pope?" he asks, this time turning his head slightly toward you, a bit threatened that someone like you could possibly know anything about music that would be new to him.

"Uh, Pope, you know," and you point to the baseball cap and he says "That's not rock n roll, that's the Pope!" and he waves his hand like he's greeting his throngs from a bulletproof Cadillac convertible "The Pope, his holiness, shoes of the fisherman."

"I don't think so. On a baseball cap?" you argue. You picture Danny adjusting the bill on the pontiff's magnificent silvery head. The Pope looking approvingly in the mirror, saying "Cool" when it's nipping just right at his forehead.

"Everyone goes for the bucks these days," he shares.

Danny walks up to the two of you and asks the boy "What do you mean-everyone? Where have you ever seen such a moment as this in your tiny lifetime?"

"I'd watch who I'm calling tiny," the kid challenges Danny.

"Yeah, yeah, nice little joke. Okay, sorry. Have you ever seen such a thing?" Danny asks.

"Never."

"Not a bad idea, huh?"

"Wouldn't buy it," the kid mutters.

Danny sighs and gets on with business.

"Would you fellows like another drink?" a very familiar gesture, nice that it isn't being aimed at you. And you exchange a glance with Danny and you know that you are not a regular – you're an insider!

"No thanks, gotta run," answers the kid.

"Maybe your friend here," pursues Danny.

"Don't know him," the kid shrugs.

You turn to the left to avoid the entire situation because this very lack of acceptance is what you come here to escape in the first place.

Thank goodness for Zeke.

"Say, you're a Catholic aren't you?" he wanders toward you and asks.

"Born a Catholic," you are pleased to answer in the affirmative.

"Well, that's very interesting. So, what do you think it felt like when Jesus first realized he was a Catholic?"

"Well, he never was a Catholic, Zeke, didn't you know that?" you can see him feeling embarrassed.

"Jesus was a Jew," you remind him.

Hey, you're glad to be talking to someone other than that despicable kid who was thankfully gone before he could tell everyone that

37

you're not worth talking to.

Downtown Toledo is absolutely booming today with the usual bunch of street people checking out the opportunities and looking downright friendly about it, like utility workers or building guards doing their rounds.

The sidewalks present their own human drama, a "Busy Bug" sort of game, the handful of big time Toledo executives scampering to their private clubs, slyly skipping around the homeless folk as if they were sandtraps on a golf course.

For some reason, the street people in Toledo are littler than those you find elsewhere, and so are their adversaries. Toledo generates a smaller kind of person for some reason, not that they aren't upstanding members of society, just that they mostly seem to be meek.

The distinction between those who live on the streets and those who consider the street a human obstacle course is quite small.

The homeless population has some quirks of its own, for example, the constant pacing, as if they were on the telephone conducting major negotiations, wearing short paths in their well-polished wooden floors. But instead of pacing ten feet here and ten feet back, they cover scads of city blocks, and it seems that you could stop most of them in their tracks and turn them the other way and they'd just keep walking, like wind-up friction toys that turn abruptly when their bumper hits an obstacle.

Is this so different than your life, you wonder? Oh, how you hate it when you find yourself looking at someone who's down and out and entertaining the notion that they prefer life to be this way. But you can't help but look at the very short jovial man bouncing by Rodeo Burger. Sure, he stops and salivates in the window, trying to make eye contact with the tall, friendly, jock type gulping down burgers and reading the want ads.

The street guy catches the customer's eye and he mimes himself eating a burger, the customer pointing to his own burger and gesturing "Mine? You want to eat my Rodeo Burger?"

The guy outside gives him a big thumbs up for having caught his drift so quickly, and then he gets across the idea that he'd like to be invited in so he can eat the burger for himself.

The customer finds this completely sensible and gestures "Why not?" He's wearing an embroidered baseball hat that says "Pope" on one line and "Harry" on the next. "Pope Harry," now wouldn't that be nice!

Chapter Eight

A week passes quickly. This one always does. Real life doesn't seem as threatening as usual, despite the rain pouring down, because nature is nothing compared to the power of that fateful choice of life-partners you made five years ago this week?

That was a lovely six months. Cupid must have been at work, taking the beautiful, alluring, educated, successful woman and turning her in to the quintessential dependent, like a puppy or a kitten but with mobility and a very big commitment to the art of purchasing. The romantic in you never looks too hard at the subjects of its attention for fear of any skepticism on your part chasing them away.

Every year around this time you find yourself wondering: "What if she really wasn't just a complainer? What if she was just so unfortunate that all of things she complained about were really true? Would I have left her then?"

You get up from your stool and begin strolling out of Danny's, nice and nonchalantly so no one knows you are stressed today. You wouldn't want them to mistake your mood as having been induced by them.

Melanie would never be caught dead in here. She would tell you that this is simply where water finds its lowest level, and she would not be surprised that you found your level here too.

You walk past the red-headed priest. You wonder why Danny doesn't collect for his drinks. You wonder why he drinks. Is this his diocese, these twenty chairs and a horse's head to pray to? You wonder why he's twirling a red silk garter belt, fondling the shiny gold embroidered letter "P" hanging from its tag like the Levi's stub on the back end of blue jeans.

But your attention is diverted by the cute young woman just outside the door. She's maybe 24. She's waving at a car going by and you're certain that she has no idea who is driving it.

Frannie, you've heard Danny call her. Must be his girl. She reminds you of Tooti-Fruiti. A canned cup of charm and innocence who a couple of dollars of makeup and a few tips from the Revlon lady over at Toledo Drug could make genuinely attractive. Before, an ordinary natural blond, a bit disheveled and a little sexy only in her apparent considerate virginity. After, a vixen constantly taking on the entire crowd.

Really, Frannie seems quite nice and definitely very cute. Could you say innocent in this day and age when everyone understands that the exchange of bodily fluids is what we once called making love?

She, like the Father, is off limits to Zeke, whose basic survival instincts make him a glutton for conversation and new acquaintances.

You walk out the door as she breezes in and you stand outside under the flimsy green awning,

scootching your jacket up around your neck to protect you from the splash of the rain. And until the
rain subsides, you look like you're watching for your
ride to pull up, but you're just listening to Frannie
who is charming the socks off everyone in her midst.

Frannie walks in almost every time you're at Danny's, but she has the kind of personality that makes
every visit feel unexpected. She gives off a sense
that several years in to a relationship with her and
she'd still be the same person you met in the first
place. Imagine that! Falling in love with someone
who is not secretly a psycho and counting off the
days until you're too committed to take off when
she reveals her true self.

At some point, simple social grace calls for you to
stick by a suffering loved one, but does this have to
apply when the main symptom of the illness is the
constant need to psychologically beat the crap out
of one's mate? If Melanie would have come down
with a lung condition or a walking problem, you'd
have nurtured her forever. But what was this thing?
Those once beaming eyes shortly after wedlock radi-
ated nothing but hate and contempt. What exactly
did she ever love about you?

Frannie seems like she'd never change on you.

But your ex, who visited the manicurist every
Wednesday to get her nicotine-stained nails coated
in unusual colors, couldn't have been sweeter or

more innocent when you first met her years ago. She was all ears.

You'd think you were reciting the biography of Herman Melville or William Shakespeare or someone big like that, but all you were telling her about was you.

"I graduated in 1967 and then I went to this Jesuit college a few miles away, studied English, and that's when I was hired by Brennan House and started proofreading recipe books, which lead to my present position of editing them, and I am somewhat well known in that field but I am genuinely a good cook as a result," you summed up your entire adult life in one careening sentence.

"Boy, you're a real achiever! I like ambitious people. I left my last boyfriend because he just wasn't ambitious, but you sure are," she said.

Maybe she and Zeke would have hit it off.

The day of your marriage and suddenly she became very ambitious herself. Ambitious to hurry on over and quit school. Quit her job. Made an appointment to get her tubes tied just to be sure there'd be no more of you in the future of civilization.

Thinking back, you figure this was not too big a sacrifice considering it would assure civilization that there'd be no more of her either.

And she spent the next two and a half years shopping for antiques and grumbling about how difficult it was to decorate a home to her standards on your income. She wolfed down stories about the pursuit of quality in magazines you'd never heard of. She would weep when you'd admit to her friends that your father was a plumber.

"You don't need to tell people that," she would angrily remind you. "Why did you marry me?" you'd ask and her instantaneous wince would reveal how much she lamented her misjudgment of you.

Still, you send her a card and flowers on your anniversary, but of course, they are no longer from a genuine florist. And every now and then you leave the price on the wrapper on purpose. She had been entertaining at one time. And it was flattering to know that someone with such good taste had selected you.

Frannie, you'd bet, would stay Frannie forever. Little things tell you so. Her constant blue jeans are the kind that are comfortable, an inch or two to spare where her butt meets her legs, kind of cute in that way for some reason. Seems the tighter the jeans in that location, the less you'd really like to work at a rapport with her.

Frannie's voice has something special about it too. The tone would be sexy if the words had any teasing forethought to them. If she seemed even the slightest bit elusive. But she's a free spirit with no agenda, a calendar with all the national holidays noted. Columbus Day was not irrelevant to her. She'd wake up that morning and take the time to be stirred by some simple memory of his fame.

You notice her rubbing her temples and you walk back in, as if she had been wishing for you.

You hear her ask Danny: "Danny what's a hypotenuse?" she reads from one of those little tiny spiral notepads which the goof ball scholars in your school used to carry in their breast pockets along with their slide rules.

"Frannie, what's with this head thing again?"

"It must be the weather," she answers.

"What's a hypotenuse have to do with your headaches or the weather?" he questions.

"It's just a word I came across that I want to know. What's so bad about self-improvement, Danny, or don't you have any room to grow?" she challenges.

"Does the sign outside say PS 101 or what? This is a b-a-r Frannie. You come here to forget that you don't know what a hypotenuse is," he explains.

"I just want to know," she answers innocently.

"What am I little old Mrs. Applethorpe and her wiggly jiggly Adam's apple?" he squeezes the little bit of skin he could grab beneath Frannie's neck.

"Ouch, Danny!" somehow her adding his name to her exclamation is nice.

And seeing how this is such a friendly place, you

feel the time has come to brave Danny's displeasure and introduce yourself.

"Hi, I'm Al," You run your fingers through the sprout of curls bursting out of the crown of your head, separated by a part on each side. You never used to have two separate parts! She looks to your hair, then to your eyes and giggles. How did she know it all used to start much lower on your forehead?

She looks at you in a somewhat welcoming way. Her eyes tell you that she pities you.

"Hi, I'm Frannie." The "hi" part is long and extended like "I'm not worthy of you." And she looks quickly to Danny and says "You know, Frannie of Frannie and Danny!" and she giggles as Danny covers his face with his hand and just groans.

"Is Frannie and Danny a marriage?" you ask.

"No, Frannie and Danny are teacher and student, trainer and pet –" and Danny grabs a nice sized pinch of Frannie's behind and adds "engine and caboose!"

"Danny, why the left side all the time, why the left side?" as she soothes the pain with the palm of her hand, not realizing how embarrassed you are that she might realize how you are fantasizing your hand doing the soothing for her.

"Al, you know I've wanted to ask you – do you think high pay is more important than liking your job?" interrupts Zeke. He must be tired. His entrance is more obsequious than usual.

Danny looks grateful as Zeke puts his arm around your neck and jerks you toward the bar. Zeke is not a subtle man, but you can't help but enjoy him pantomiming a subtle character.

"A hypotenuse is the sum of the two rays facing the largest angle," you turn your head back toward Frannie and answer her original question.

She giggles. Danny looks quizzically at you with that same look that always makes you feel tired. "Thanks, and geeze, you're smart!" she says and lifts her chin up at Danny. "Bye bye butterfly!" On her way out she shares a genuine little smile with you.

The smile feels real out of place here. Your ex-wife had that same sort of innocent laugh, just like Frannie, but it only appeared when you gave her things.

And to this day, you can't help but keep in some sort of touch. For the benefit of the doubt. Just in case that swelling she always felt in her uterus was actually more than a call for attention.

That night, you're grieving over how awkward
your furniture looks and agonizing over how three
days could go by without a single message on your
answering machine. You change the greeting once
again, beseeching the caller to leave word. "I'm really sorry I can't be here to answer your call personally, but I'll make up for it as soon as I return."

What a mess! Why can't you set a single thing
down where it really belongs? Your life is one thing
after another out of place, just a bit off kilter.
Melanie could take a shoe box and set it down pre-
cisely where it works best. It would take on a prominence in the dining room. You can't make your dining room look like it belongs there.

Danny and Frannie are at her place, and you can
imagine them in front of a live audience playing the
role of a cheery, kooky couple, still children flailing
around in grown up bodies. Playful cats tripping on
their own adult nails, wondering where such serious
tools came from.

"Ever notice that the customers don't talk much
to each other at your place, Danny?" she asks. "If
Zeke or you don't talk, it's like you took the batteries
out of the real customers," she comments.

"They don't think you're for real. I heard that Al
guy say he can't imagine that you ever sleep," she
whispers.

"Sleep is a waste of time. I hate unconsciousness," Danny proclaims.

He stares at the pendulum darting back and forth on the cheap purple plastic clock mounted sloppily on her bedroom wall. Of course, the pendulum is completely disassociated with the clock movement, so it's always out of synch with the second hand, but Danny never finds this disturbing. It's the only clock in her little dainty but oddly disheveled apartment.

"There aren't enough hours in the day as it is. I have to make some serious money. I feel like a woman right at the edge of her child-bearing years, and all I've done is a little French kissing," he complains.

"Oh, is that how you view our relationship?" she turns toward him.

"I mean I haven't used my potential," he pats the back of her hair and she quickly becomes gentle again.

"You know that I believe in your potential, don't you?" she says.

"The bar loses money. I could lose it. But I need a base of operations, a place to do business from. Gotta make something hit now," he confides.

No one knows that he hasn't paid any rent for months and that every few nights he refills most of the liquor bottles from somewhat lesser brands, no easy feat considering how tough it is to find cheaper brands than what he admits to be serving.

"Hit what?"

"The deal I'm working on for the Pope, for one."

"You are working for the Pope?" she is incredulous.

"Not for the Pope. With the Pope. The plan goes to him tomorrow," Danny reports.

"That's very impressive," she answers.

"And if he doesn't bite, I'm moving on to something even bigger," he answers.

"The Pope is pretty high up," she reminds him.

"Well, then, he ought to know how to play ball with the big boys," Danny mutters.

Frannie knows that this would be the perfect time for lovemaking, which he only shared with her a couple of times, not because he isn't attracted, but mostly because this wasn't the kind of woman he wanted to do that sort of thing with.

There were other kinds for that when you needed it. He liked and respected her too much.

Earlier on, he couldn't contain his lust for her. She gave herself to him after months of keeping him at bay. He admired her for this. Everything about him was short when it came to anything but intellectual exchange.

"Well, then if you have a bigger idea, do that one too, no matter what the Pope says," she advises. "You aren't going to put your life on hold waiting for the Pope, I hope!" she exclaims.

"My word is my bond. I've got to be ready to move if he goes for the deal."

"I know that, Danny, but you should be ready if he doesn't, just in case."

"I'm ready," he turns to her and she knows he has a backup plan.

"The Pope's chopped liver compared to Plan B." Frannie knows that Danny is not kidding.

"I'm not running a bar for my beauty," he says seriously and then breaks in to laughter when she answers "Oh, really," in that special sarcastic way that reveals how much smarter she is than him in an intuitive way.

"I know that whatever you do is going to be legitimate, right?" she asks.

"Oh, absolutely!"

Frannie takes off for the bathroom and Danny swats her butt on the way.

"You make my head hurt sometimes," she complains as she closes the door behind her.

"You should get that checked," he yells.

"I should get you checked!" she screeches.

"You're the disease. I'm just the symptom!!!" she adds.

Danny lets the moment pass. Headaches, headaches, constant headaches. His feeling is that everybody always has something that's not exactly right. Some are so inwardly absorbed, they can't even overlook a simple headache. Others, like him, are too busy with outside things. At the moment, Danny is fantasizing about Plan B, but in his heart of hearts, he knows that the Pope idea is a bit more realistic in an execution sense.

"Hey I got you a present!" Danny announces out of nowhere, and Frannie's head instantly cranes around the white wooden door where she's sitting on the can doing nothing but taking a magazine test to see how stirring she is to men.

Danny pulls his "Day of Truth" gym bag out from under the bed. She groans as she remembers that bag. Another goofy idea from when they first met, Danny renting the Toledo Arena for a show he called Day of Truth. He paraded a dozen or so infamous cult leaders on stage to tell the truth as they so firmly believed it. And no one objected too much, because the only people there were those who had already been indoctrinated, which, luckily for Danny, filled enough seats for him to go back to Talk of the Town without having to give the key to any creditors.

"What, Danny?" she asks excitedly.

"Look here," and he takes a frilly little red and black silky bra out and hands it to her.

"Pope" on one side, "Toledo" on the other. She studies the words.

"This is your Pope plan?" she asks dryly.

"It's just a joke derived from it," he urges.

"You and your sewing computer!" she jokes.

"Why not? It's just sitting there waiting for the landlord to send it back to whoever financed it, and he appreciates me storing it for him," Danny explains.

"So you decided to do something religious with it, huh?" she laughs as she straps the bra on over her sweatshirt.

"Hey, religion is where the heart is," he responds, his fingers snapping the bra strap, and it breaks where the cups meet.

"Cheap," says Frannie.

"Minuscule" says Danny as he playfully grabs her tiny bosoms.

"Anything more than a mouthful –" she says jokingly, but forgets how it ends. "What's this all about?" she asks.

"It's something me and Father Mulroy have been talking about," he gets serious again.

"We're presenting it tomorrow," he looks to her for a sign of interest but she's busy displaying her shapely legs to the mirror. He wonders if women know what they do to men. If they are calculating every move, watching for reaction out of the corners of their eyes. Or, more likely he figures, maybe those with the best body parts are missing the brain parts that give a person such insight.

"Presenting embroidered brassieres to the nuns?"
she giggles. "I don't know if they wear them. Never
saw titty-bumps on a nun," she ponders.

"Hey, the Pope's got eyes!!!" he jokes.

"And matching jockstraps for the priests?"

"They've got equipment too," he laughs.

"What does Father Mulroy say about this?" she
asks.

"He's getting me an introduction. We're taking
the collection to his old church, to Father Pat. The
one who took over," he says seriously.

She knows better than to ask too much right now.
Silly or not, she thinks someday one of Danny's
schemes will actually work. He's a monkey eternally
poking at the keyboard.

And every now and then the good Lord will give a
wink and a nod to a silly idea and let it work just to
give everyone else a bit of hope. That's what separates genius from buffoonery in Danny's mind.

Chapter Ten

The little feet walk big. They are proud of their shine. The church's few remaining stained glass windows glare their once bright colors off the black wing tips. Danny DeMarco is on the mission. He's at the helm of a nuclear, laser-guided enemy submarine, periscope up full, ripping its way through the floor, the captain working under the insane notion that no one knows he's coming.

The footsteps echo through the empty chapel. Father Mulroy is at his side, but his tennis shoes are not contributing to the optimistic and strident echoes. Danny DeMarco could use some offsetting influence right now, saluting his positive attitude in his reflection off the shiny crystal of his fake Rolex watch.

"Where are we going?" Danny mutters quietly so his feet don't get wind of his uncertainty.

"The anteroom. He's waiting," answers Father Mulroy just as softly.

"What's his state of mind?" Danny asks, sounding like an ad agency president revving up, thinking he's Al Pacino sinking in to a special character he devised just for this audience.

"Brimstone," the Father mutters.

"Brimstone?" Danny echoes.

"He's like an old wool sweater, the oily kind made with big, thick yarn."

"He's a patent leather wallet to me," Danny counters.

"An empty one," says Mulroy as they approach the big wooden door that needed to be sanded and stained several decades ago.

"Well, say a prayer," Danny knocks firmly on the door. He hears a tired man's voice reply "Hello," and, disappointed that someone so close to the Lord doesn't sound a bit more commanding, Danny flips his red on blue polka-dot tie off his shoulder. Father Mulroy looks to the heavens and says "I'm sorry," silently, and they enter the dusty room lighted only by a few lost sunrays trying to find their way out.

Ever since Father Mulroy's mysterious passing from the pulpit, St. Matts Christian Hall had lost its electricity. Figuratively and literally. No money. No charisma. Its few parishioners figured it had something to do with dogma, a slight disagreement on some aspect of worship that Bishop Flagg had up his butt, but the pragmatic Father Mulroy had run out of patience and diplomacy. No one knows for sure.

Was it the singing in Latin? There was no suspicion of the ugly kind of crimes too often associated with defrocked members of the clergy. This had to be an ego thing, the kind of mess that is personal, just between the guys. In fact, what's the big surprise? These kind of things are to be expected among guys who believe they stand taller in the sky than the regular folk.

Old Father Pat was assigned in Father Mulroy's place, and there was no resentment between them. Bishop Flagg left the place alone these days. Even in a small religion, St. Matt's wouldn't have been a consequential prayer establishment. Its worn down wood and crackly floors, its shaky pews and grimy little chapel wouldn't serve any form of belief proudly.

There were a number of statues and idols as one would expect, except to this day, no one could figure out who or what any of them represent. From day one, this church couldn't have been expected to amount to much.

"Father Pat, this is Mr. DeMarco," Father Mulroy introduces Danny to the frail, tall man perched over a lectern, looking up from an old issue of Popular Science opened to one of those Edmund Scientific ads, the picture of an ant farm circled in red.

For a moment, Danny is lost in a worry that maybe Frannie's headaches are coming a bit too often.

"A distinct pleasure, Father Pat," Danny greets the tired Father. Danny notices that Father Pat's gums are receding in oval pattern much like the head of the monk on the bottle of Benedictine liquor.

"I was thinking of ordering this. Do you remember it?" Father Pat asks Mulroy and Danny.

Danny looks at the yellowed pages on the magazine, first noticing that it's only several months old, then wondering if he is aging this quickly just by standing there.

"They send you the ants separately, and if one of them is from a different colony, he eats them all, or something," Danny offers, remembering that Frannie's brother Harry has something to do with ants.

"Oh," mutters Father Pat. "How will I know if one doesn't belong?" he asks.

"He'll have another ant hanging out of his mouth," Danny jokes, but the old priest just picks up the magazine and studies it closer, looking for an assurance that this won't be a depressing purchase.

"Maybe we can do Father Pat a favor and find out more for him," suggests Father Mulroy.

The similarities shared by the two fathers are quite striking. One red hair, the other whisky brown, but both limp. Tired skin. One looks like he long ago gave up drinking, the other long ago started. They both learned to believe in all the various church things, and each no longer worries that most of it just might have been a bit misleading.

It's not the truth of things that matters any more. It's the conviction. If you really, truly believe in something that you know is invalid, that's called faith. Faith feels good. They can both live on that.

"Yeah, I can get you stuff on the ants. My sort-of

brother-in-law knows all that. But, reality first, so let's get down to business," Danny replies, and with a flick of the wrist an aluminum chart rack unfolds and stands wobbly on the uneven wooden planks. He opens his fake Zero Haliburton aluminum briefcase and unrolls a display pad of paper and attaches it to the frame.

"Yes, you have material to discuss," Father Pat confirms.

Danny reaches in his pocket and yanks out his key ring, gripping the little red metal flashlight attached to it, turns it on and pans his tiny spotlight across the title page which reads "THE MISSING MARK."

Father Pat glances toward his Popular Science magazine and considers whether it would be all that bad if one ant did eat the rest, and what might happen if he dropped a little church cockroach in, just as a sociological study.

"What we have here is a lesson to be learned about the way people think," begins Danny. "And we uncover the missing mark, an opportunity to fill a need and, of course, generate what I imagine is severely needed income." He looks around and sniffs with displeasure at the environment like he's in the zoo.

He flips the page with great flourish.

"Of course," adds Father Mulroy, his eyes completely glazed.

"Now, Father Pat, or do you prefer Patrick, or what?" Danny interrupts.

"I like Pat. It feels like a Boy's Town kind of priest," he exposes a hungry little smile.

"What we are seeking here today is a unification of church and business all in the name of prosperity, which means freedom, which means time, which means Sunday isn't the only day anymore for fun, and that results in people at Church, you follow?" Danny shifts in to second gear.

Father Pat flourishes his hand in the air for no particular reason. It's a caretaker's hand. Fingernails rounded even though they'd never seen a nail file, much less a manicurist.

Danny turns the page to reveal a bar chart. There are five bars, the first four rising evenly about half way up the paper. Under the first is the title ROLLING STONES. Followed under the rest by ELVIS, BEATLES, BEACH BOYS and MADONNA. The next one rises through the top of the paper. Under it is printed in bolder capital letters: THE POPE.

"These are attendance figures for the last calendar year. The top five draws touring the world today. As you can see, the Pope has no equal. More people see him when he sticks his head out the window over the Vatican than attend every concert in America on any given night."

"I see," says the Father, gazing directly at Danny, wondering if that big spider web in the corner over his easel would inevitably engulf the little man if his presentation goes on beyond nap time.

Danny turns the chart to the next page which features the same five titles under a series of bar charts, this time with all the others rising to the top of the page, while the one labeled THE POPE does not rise at all.

"These are merchandising income," Danny states solemnly .

"Merchandising," reverberates Father Pat.

"Merchandising. Right now the Pope sells nothing," Danny reports as he reaches in his case and pulls out an assortment of colorful items, gesturing to Father Mulroy to help display them on the metal shelf hanging by a thread to the wall beside them. Each is emblazoned with a diamond-shaped gold, silver and bright blue embroidered emblem that says POPE ON TOUR, and adds in smaller letters POPE WORLD TOUR, and lists a variety of cities throughout the nation with dates next to them.

"T-Shirts, very popular, one in five buy them, $18 each, easy, up to $25 depending on the design, no problem," Danny rattles off the data like a Gatling gun, the Father's head wobbling like a slow motion print head on one of those old IBM Selectric typewriters.

"Sweatshirts, same story, a buck more in cost, 50% more in selling price – caps, bags, sweat bands, souvenir booklets – you can go far as the imagination allows" Danny is on a roll. He pulls out the red garter belt and pledges solemnly to Father Pat. "As far as you want to go."

Danny turns the page and reveals a single number.

He recites it as he flashes his red light on one digit at a time. One. Three. Four. Zero. Zero. Zero. Zero. Zero. Zero. Etcetera. Get the point, Father. One point three. Eight zeros. Billion. Tell him Father Mulroy," and he turns his head to his red-headed friend so his little intense pupils don't have to move, which at this point of his intensity might cause an internal meltdown within his skull.

"One point three billion dollars is what he is saying," Father Mulroy says calmly.

"I will take it in to consideration, Father Mulroy." The man is either very wise or is presently elsewhere, having forgotten to take his body along for the ride.

"This is a matter of the highest resoluteness," Danny speaks solemnly, his hands out before him, fingers spread. He pauses for a moment wondering what 'resolute' actually means, but figuring his tone gets the message across, he continues "You must present this to the Pope himself."

"Okay," the Father answers obediently. "I will. Can you leave the presentation?"

Danny beams proudly to Father Mulroy, and appreciatively says to the old priest: "Certainly, and you can keep these after your presentation. They're limited editions," and he thanks the priest for his time and asks one last question: "When would it be appropriate to call you back for the answer, Father?"

"Tomorrow," he responds positively.

Father Mulroy lifts his eyes to the heavens without moving his face.

"Tomorrow it is. Thank you," and Danny shuts his case, wishing he had purchased the real Zero Haliburton because he knew its spaceship sounding click and seal would have felt just perfect right now. That's how locked up he knew this deal was becoming.

"Mr. DeMarco!" the Priest's voice sounds more enthusiastic as he stops him at the door.

"Could you find out about the ants?" he asks meekly.

"The ants?" Danny turns his head to Father Mulroy.

"The ant farm," Father Mulroy reminds him.

"Oh, the ant farm, sure, no problem, I'll call Harry."

And he walks big, once again. Bigger than ever.

The Pope. Danny DeMarco, world-exclusive licensee. The ultimate brand name. He could see well beyond the kiosks set up at every stop where the Pontiff's car will cruise. He could see restaurants. Bookstores. Amusement Parks. He could imagine Pope cereals. Pope ashtrays.

Who needs a Plan B when Plan A is so perfect!

Even Father Mulroy didn't know how open Bishop Flagg might be to this suggestion. More at issue here would be Father Pat's attention span. There is a distinct possibility that the matter has already been forgotten.

Danny would want them to cut through the intermediaries and go directly to the Pope. Of course, Danny didn't understand that the Pope is no more in charge of the Catholic Church than the President is in charge of the nation.

There have been many Popes and Presidents. You have to focus not on who comes and goes but who stays.

The Bishop Flaggs, the Bishop Hutts, they are the ones. The Pope has a very nice way about him and does a nice job holding the whole thing together spiritually. The decision-makers are not the policy-makers. Policy is a silly exercise in self-importance. The Pope does not change the direction of the Church because if he would be inclined to do such a thing, he never would have been chosen in the first place.

"Hey, you wanna call your place holy, you want the name, you gotta call Danny DeMarco." He can hear one of the Pope's key guys setting some potential sub-licensee straight while talking loudly over his sculpted gold handset.

"You want the Pope, you gotta call Danny. You can't get around him!" he loved the sound of those words.

They change venue to John's Diner, a railroad car kind of place that never bothered trying to distinguish itself as anything more than a cup of coffee and an air of hospitality that was more patient than friendly.

"I think it went well, very well, but do you think he has the juice?" Danny asks the Father.

"The Jews?" Mulroy is mildly startled. There were Jews in Toledo but none who could help him figure out how to catch up with the Pope.

"Juice, like orange and grapefruit!" Danny exclaims.

"I don't know if he has any juice. What does that have to do with it?" the Father is confused.

"I'm talking about greasing the tracks, are we with a guy who can get us through the right doors? I have my concerns," Danny admits.

"I don't know that the Pope himself would accept his call, but perhaps that is not necessary for your success," Mulroy calmly explains. Mulroy was always calm. As Danny's glance tired its subject, Mulroy's soothed. This seemed to be a man who has inadvertently caused some harm when none was intended, and he's constantly trying to make amends.

"You've told me that St. Matt's once was the Talk of the Town, no pun intended, but what's the big secret about why you aren't there anymore?" Danny asks as the large-legged waitress stomps to the table spilling both the coffees on each of her feet.

"A labor of love," he jokes to Mulroy as he nods toward the plodding server.

"Anything else?" she asks as she sets down the half cups of very black fluid. Mulroy notices that she is breathing hard.

"No, but thank you," he answers politely.

"Yeah, could you bring me a telephone?" Danny asks with a sparkle in his eyes.

Her uninterested eyes answered both negatively and unamused.

"How about a telephone book?" he comes back for more.

"It's chained to the phone over there," she gestures to the entrance.

"Could I have a glass of ice water then?" Danny is nodding his head and puckering up his chin in quiet glee.

She looks to the water fountain half a dozen seats away and behind the grainy pink Formica counter, expels a sorrowful sigh, and silently turns and plods to fulfill the undeniable request.

"You should be more thoughtful," says Father Mulroy.

"I don't like her attitude. You know right off that she resents doing anything for you. Don't you recognize that?" Danny asks.

"I doubt that this is what she wants to be doing," Mulroy answers solemnly.

"If she acted like a content person, she'd be content. I selected from being content or being discontent and chose content. It's that simple," Danny gloats. "Life is a matter of options."

"I chose to lose the church," Mulroy throws a quiet curve ball.

"Good decision," Danny says sarcastically.

"Here's your water, anything else?" the waitress has tried on a new attitude as if she had overheard them and is experimenting with her own body language.

"Let me ask you something," Danny suggests and she maintains her new composure to the extent that she doesn't walk away immediately.

"What?" she answers half-heartedly.

"How important is this job to you?" he looks toward Mulroy as he sets his stage with the waitress.

"This ain't what I do for a living, it's just some extra," she replies.

"What do you really do?" he looks to Mulroy then to her and adds "Psychiatry?"

"Investments," she answers.

"Investments," he mutters in disbelief.

"Here's my card," it jumps out of her sleeve like an Ace of Spades.

"If you ever need a resource," she adds.

"I could use some sugar for my coffee," Danny says playfully.

"I've got a sort of history where your bar is," she continues.

"Oh yeah? Lots of women have a history over there," says Danny.

"I mean the guy who used to be in your space, he's a client of mine."

"What became of him?" Danny asks.

"Wealthiest motherfucker in Argentina who's not a Nazi," she proclaims, adding "I'm not saying there are no Nazi's in his bridge games, mind you."

"That so? Well, if you see your client, remind him that he left his embroidery machine behind and I want some storage money," Danny laughs as he glances down at her ragged business card.

"Dolores Irons, Personal Investment Counselor." Very spunky. Very spunky." Danny pockets the card. "Sounds like a wrestler," he says to her. She rolls her eyes, then trudges away.

"I'm going to see the wrestling show tomorrow

night, wanna come?" Danny moves on and is surprised that Mulroy can keep up with his ever changing interests, points of view and attitudes.

"You have tickets?" the Father asks.

"Yeah, three."

"I can't," the Father answers as he looks toward the waitress. She's talking to the young black cook who is carefully shoving tuna in a pita bread with his finger.

"Okay, well then, will you stick around at the place, cause I was thinking of maybe taking Zeke and that guy Al," says Danny.

"If you were thinking of taking them, why did you ask me?" Mulroy asks more rhetorically than as if he cares.

"Because I don't hardly know Al and I don't hardly have an interest in Zeke, so you should come first, but I knew you don't appreciate the sport, but I had to ask you first." Danny reveals his odd sense of balance which Mulroy no longer bothers trying to comprehend.

"I don't mind," concludes Mulroy. "Who'll be tending bar?"

"Frannie," Danny says with a glisten.

"Frannie? Your Frannie?" Mulroy is surprised.

"I need someone besides you at the phone," answers Danny, "Just in case he calls."

"Father Pat?"

"No, the Pope," Danny answers dryly. "He's gonna call or that Bishop's gonna call, and no offense, but how would they like it if you was the one who answered?"

"He wouldn't know."

"He'd know." Danny ends the conversation and wrestles for a moment with the possibility of Dolores Irons and her investment consultation firm being just ridiculous enough to fit in to his life at some time.

"Do you really think so?" Mulroy asks the air.

"You think they make you Pope for being stupid?" "These are very smart people," he replies. "Conniving!" "The church is the McDonalds of religion," he praises.

**Chapter
Eleven**

"I know this is inappropriate, Father, but I don't view myself as the person to make judgments on these matters." Father Pat speaks slowly and humbly to Bishop Flagg.

"It would raise needed funds for repairs. We could have hot water more often," he adds.

"Father, I appreciate your discomfort and I take comfort in your earnestness." Bishop Flagg is not an impatient man, but this particular diocese is a real yawner to him.

"I understand that it would be done in the best of taste," Father Pat labors.

"Yes, yes, of course, of course," the Bishop is playing with the rheostat on his new 12 volt suspended halogen lighting system.

"Hats and T-Shirts and the like," the Father blurts.

"With the Pope's likeness," he quickly summarizes.

"Souvenirs. And from this you would raise money for various local needs and affairs?" the Bishop helps him get on with it.

"Yes."

"To the tune of..." the Bishop asks for a dollar amount.

"One point three billion."

"One point three billion. Dollars?"

"Yes, this is what has been projected apparently, but..."

The Bishop turns the light up full and takes his gold, limited edition Mont Blanc pen in hand and writes: Pope memorabilia.

"I will pass your idea on to others. It is very difficult ground, you know," he says to the old Father.

"I understand," Father Pat says with reverence.

"Do you have this down on paper?" asks the Bishop.

"Yes, I do."

"Get it to me please."

"I will."

We'll be back." And Bishop Flagg presses the mother of pearl button on his desktop, signaling his secretary that he requires the luncheon menu post haste.

Chapter Twelve

"Zeke, wrestling tomorrow night?" Danny puts it to Zeke as an instruction rather than an invitation. Zeke, quick to be affirmative, shakes his head. You picture him in ceramic white with a cheap spring connecting his head to his shoulders with a spot of rubber cement holding him to the dashboard.

"How about you, Al?" he looks toward you like it's presumed that you, Zeke and he are a threesome for the event. This is very gratifying. You've now invested numerous visits to the place, and are striving toward becoming a fixture.

It pleases you to be treated as an appendage to this Talk of the Town.

"Me, what?" you ask, wondering if something is happening here which is ultimately going to scare you away.

"Wrestling! Hank the Tank and The Ultimate Terror fighting for the world title! Coming?" Danny is very buoyant, somewhat bloated by his own generosity. "Tickets are on me." He got them for free from that Asian girl who sells radio time during the day and who trusts Danny to keep a secret about her evenings.

"Yeah, sure, thanks, I'd love to," you can't recall having been invited to be one of the boys ever in your life. In school, you were only included if you happened to be around when an event was being considered and it would be too outlandishly rude to exclude you.

You think that wrestling is idiotic and you hope you'll stand out as someone who just came for the diversion. But no one invites you to the orchestra or ballet, so maybe this is where you belong. Maybe these are your people. Maybe you don't stand out.

You are the one of the wrestling crowd. The joke is on everyone else! You've finished the asparagus book and are on to a Russian appetizer deal. You have a certain sophistication even if it's well hidden.

"Zeke, I'm putting you temporarily in charge tonight. Al, can you give me a lift?" Danny addresses you and the other member of the boys. You feel elevated. He likes you. He needs you. You can do something for him. Why does this feel glorious?

"A ride, Al, do you mind?" he asks again.

"Sure, where do you need to go?" you jump so quickly to the call that you spill the head off your brew, but it's still foaming so you blow it right off your lap and on to the floor.

"To the Turnpike, that's all, do you mind?" Danny asks as he notices the slight dampness on the floor and instead of looking to you, he turns his head to Zeke and cocks his chin toward the mop. "I said you're in charge," he reminds Zeke who can't decide whether to be proud or humiliated.

"Thanks, I guess," Zeke replies forlornly.

"And when Al gets back, let him do the talking,

and you can pour." Danny tosses out his directions to Zeke.

You wonder if you'd feel comfortable doing your recipe book editing here between customers. This could become a way of life. Imagine a life with people in it! It's been a long time since all your friends abandoned you because Melanie told you it was time to choose.

Zeke rushes for the mop and slops away the beer foam while you rush out the door. "I'll get the car and pull out front for you." You dash off like an excited school boy celebrating his first inexplicable hard-on.

In your frenzy, you leave behind the anniversary card you just filled out for Melanie. Danny reaches for it and walks slowly toward the door, touched by the glance he's stolen at your private message.

My days are like a shadow that declineth and I am withered like grass. There is a time to kill, a time to heal; a time to break down, and a time to build up. Happy Anniversary.

He doesn't realize that you still hate her. A little chill runs down his arm but quickly passes. He hates that he has such feelings from time to time. To him, it's like a symptom of yellow fever.

The cover of the card is a watercolor of a beautiful Persian rug with a little white cat purring over how lovely life could be if one accepts things at face value and only absorbs the truth when it is pleasant.

"I didn't know you were a religious man," Danny comments as he gets in your four-door, 'I'm a no-body' Chevy and hands you the card.

"You forgot this. I thought it was mine. Sorry I read it," he apologizes with a wave of his hand that tells you he feels perfectly entitled to read what he wants. You consider this a good sign. He is being thoughtful even though you are at this moment not officially a paying customer.

"I used to be. Still read the Bible, but just because I always find a better way of saying things," you explain.

"Like a greeting card, I mean, all I'd come up with on my own is 'If I had been able to put up with you, today would be our anniversary,' which is not poetic at all," you add. "I'm no Robert Frost or e.e. cummings," as if he doesn't know.

And Danny has heard enough.

"Oh, well, you know where all the motels are by the Turnpike?" he asks.

"Sure, just name your destination. Arise and let us flee!" you bellow like a tipsy choir boy who had snuck a few too many sips of holy beverage.

"I know that one," Danny claims, always the game man. "Spartacus," he declares. You can almost hear the farting buzzer proclaiming him wrong.

"Sorry, you lose. It's Samuel! chapter 15, verse

14." Danny's pride is dashed, but just for a second.

"Samuel, uh, and Delilah, yeah. That's what I meant to say." He tosses his error off. Then a burst of devilish brightness overwhelms him and his manic pupils aim his head in the direction of his crotch. "Arise! Arise!!!" he instructs his erogenous zone loud enough to penetrate the fold of stomach blocking a direct route.

"I'd arise 24 hours a day for her." He has totally confused you.

"The slut!" he spits toward the sky.

"You've never read the Bible, have you Danny?" you ask nicely.

"I know the Bible! I wrote the Bible on the Bible!!" Danny exclaims.

"What?" you ask.

"What the Bible pretends to understand is my personal specialty. Hope in the face of tragedy. I on the other hand do not even acknowledge the existence of tragedy. You see the devil. I see Jesus. Jesus in you. Jesus in me. Jesus in everyone who walks in the door. I don't even hear tragedy knocking," he goes on and on possessed with something that is somehow not blasphemous.

"I am God," you declare rhetorically. "The three biggest words, that's what you're saying? We are all God together?" you surmise for him.

"God, Jesus, Mohammed, Samson, Hoover,

Kennedy, Ford, Colonel Sanders, all the same, just big juicy images wrapping their enormous arms around us so we don't have to be afraid of death."

"They're only thoughts, Danny, they aren't flesh and blood," you remind him.

"Exactly, even as ideas you can't kill them. You've gotta grasp them. Hug 'em, shield yourself with them. They last forever. Stick with them and you might too!" he explains.

"Colonel Sanders does not make me feel comfortable with dying, Danny," you gently retort.

"There is no death!!!! I deny it!!! I defy it!!!! I am bigger than Colonel Sanders. I've blocked the possibilities. I chose to. I won't die!!!" He is bumping his head against the roof of the car and the courtesy light flickers with every bounce.

"You deny death," is all you can say.

Danny looks to the sky and beckons the spirits with his arms. "Reveal yourself to me even if you have to strike me dead right this second!" You are aghast. His death seems imminent. You're at least that much of a believer. You don't even want to be sitting next to him right now, just in case the Lord is a little off when aims his wrath at the little madman.

"As long as I am doing something big, I am invincible. Anything else and you're a sitting duck," he concludes, then looks away and you know this conversation is mercifully over.

"Over there" he points toward a phone booth standing like a banished soldier, left to guard the closed-down 25 Cent Car Wash, a one-overhang little drive-thru where for a quarter you slop heavy and sticky suds all over your car and have to spend the next $3.00 in quarters to rinse them all off.

Adjacent to that is a tiny office surrounded by a handful of sleepy rental cottages.

"You'll be going back to the place?" he suggests very strongly, again a good sign that he considers the bar incomplete without you.

"Yeah, sure am Danny."

"I'll call you there if I need a ride back," he states as a matter of how things are between you and him.

"And first one's on me tomorrow," Danny promises as he exits the car and slams the door like he's a man and a half bigger than he really stands. But this is a good little drive for you because just like Father Mulroy, you might actually be a friend.

"Hey, you know what to do at the place?" Danny stands on his toes and thrusts as much of his head in the window as possible.

"Yeah, sure, talk to the people," you agree.

"Make them feel at home," he instructs.

You picture a huge Trojan horse with Danny's face sloppily attached at the neck, him conjuring up all sorts of crazy images now colliding inside your head.

"Deny tragedy. Deny loneliness. Deny what is. Deny that you have no mate."

For a second this feels like one of those pre-dawn black car scenes at the side of a country road. Your best old friend from the gang explaining some realities of life that have escaped you. Out of nowhere, he kisses you on the lips and a dwarfish little mug in the back seat shoots a hole in your head.

"Now if the Pope or anyone religious calls, just be businesslike. Tell them I'm out on a consultation," Danny finalizes the plan.

"No problem," you promise. You feel like you're dropping someone off at the airport, not at a phone booth in the middle of nowhere.

"You and Zeke could end up smelling real good if things work out the way I expect. Commissions. Piece of the action. Do they give you a piece of the action at the cookbook joint?" he is tapping his thumbnail on the chrome window panel.

"No, I just get free copies," you answer. Cookbooks are to cooks like tennis shoes are to sports. Most of them are just for show. But your recipes actually do work for those who bother going beyond the pictures to satisfy their appetites.

"Thanks for the ride. If it's slow and you want to talk Bible, Father Mulroy's always open for business," he concludes with a soft laugh.

Danny lumbers away like he's on his way to do

something sad. He carries his quarter to the phone booth like it's an offering. You start slowly driving away, keeping an eye on him in your mirror.

The ramshackle booth casts a sad yellow kind of glow as Danny opens the door. He's reflecting the dirty neon tube above him, but the reflection seems brighter than the source.

"Thank you for getting back to me so soon, Bishop Flagg." Father Pat is genuinely taken by the attention. Why didn't they call as quickly about the phone going out? Where were they during the winter when the chapel started becoming a shelter?

There's been an extended family of wounded crashing there nightly since then. He doesn't even notice anymore, preferring to view them as his congregation.

Last Sunday, there were the 30 or so of them and one neighborhood lady, a Mrs. Crasko, who finds the little tubby one adorable and is wooing him with red licorice.

"How are you, Father?" the Bishop asks while he flips through the new AD AGE magazine, checking out the lingering success of Rambo merchandise. He was enjoying a new kind of revelation, that people are so desperate for identity that they embrace anything that's bigger than they are, as if someone else's presence can become their own.

As if people don't immediately size you up and realize that you aren't a famous basketball player or movie star. Nevertheless, he has realized that very few people have enough self-esteem to feel truly positive about themselves, so they are perfectly happy to purchase an affiliation with others.

"I have news. Unfortunately my news is not good," the Bishop speaks blandly to Father Pat, who is still dazzled that the Church even pestered return-ing his call.

"We don't find this marketing idea appropriate. Maybe you should try a bake sale," the Bishop sounds very apologetic.

Danny is standing in the phone booth across from the Turnpike exit. His feet are crunching in to remnants of last night's July 4th fireworks when, apparently, several of Toledo's finest decided to try and launch this particular phone booth.

"I can't be with you tonight cause I'm waiting for the call," explains Danny to Frannie. A thousand motel rooms beckon him. He enjoys fantasizing about opening day at the defunct car wash, another ignorant wishful thinker on his way to bankruptcy.

"Danny, I think you're dreaming," she cautions him.

"It's not a dream!" he answers.

"Well, should I pack my bags for the tour?" she asks innocently, like a rose asking if it should bloom, not realizing that it has no say in the matter.

"Cross your fingers. There wasn't much of an audience, just one priest, but he was old so he probably has a great deal of clout," Danny explains.

"Was he old and feeble or old and spunky?" she asks.

"He wanted to know about raising ants," he sighs "so I lean toward feeble, with a possible side order of goof ball."

"You could ask Harry," she reminds him.

"Harry. I thought of him. Just what I need," he mutters, wondering why this gentle brother who bores him has somehow become part of his greatest business idea ever. How would he explain Harry during his interview with Billboard? Harry doesn't have the motivation of an ant.

"Danny, Harry counts just like you do, so don't use that tone when you talk about my brother. Why, the way he treats those ants, well, they have hearts and souls just like you," she admonishes him.

"Bigger hearts and better souls!!" she continues.

"You're comparing my heart and soul to those of an ant?"

"I wouldn't insult them like that," she sighs.

The truth was that Harry Hamilton was misunderstood. He'd walk through the streets in the middle of the day like a shepherd rounding up his flock of innocents and remnants of the town's betrayal, or so they'd claim to be.

You might find Harry sitting on the stoop in the slim little alley separating Toledo Drug from Short Hairs, the all-girl barber shop where JoAnne Conroy and Beth Karol would strive to be as stylish as they could get away with.

Harry would be more likely to be sharing a cup of cold coffee left over from having ordered the Mighty Jumbo instead of the King Sized since it's just a dime more at the quick stop place on Elm. He'd be sharing it with some down and out kid who dropped out of school and who has justified everyone's decision to give up on him.

Harry was a very respectable fellow to be seen with except it never appeared that way because of who he was always seen with. Always the ones in trouble. His front porch always a destination for those who had no where to go but wanted to seem on the way to somewhere.

Harry was just a guy who wandered a lot.

He wandered. He lingered. He seemed to think a lot but no one was sure of his level of wisdom. He certainly didn't push it on anyone over at Rodeo Burger where he'd be having his nightly burger and fries with that gritty kind of brownish yellow mustard he'd bring with him in those little silver packets that looked like they came from France.

And Harry would never picture his baby sister talking away with some arm-flailing little shyster pretending to be home but calling from the edge of promiscuity where the truck drivers dragged half drunk girls into the backs of their coaches, dropping them to the ground a few moments later with a few dirty and sadly earned dollars in their weakened hands.

"Arise and let us flee!" Danny laughs as he raises his arms to the heavens, a view which at the moment is dominated by a broken fan and the dirty neon tube half covered with mosquitoes that tried in vain to suck out its gasses.

"Where are we fleeing to," she asks curiously, not

realizing that he's just having fun being a TV preacher for a moment, and he remembers "Brimstone" and not sure of what it is, decides that it's the kind of word that doesn't matter what it means.

Not hearing a response, she says "I was going to really let you be with me tonight, Danny, in the Bible sense." She giggles, knowing that this would be of no interest to either of them one way or another, except in concept form. They both enjoy the titillation of lovemaking, but they find themselves laughing shortly after actually engaging in it.

"Well, listen though, I wanted to tell you, I've got to talk to Harry," he counters.

"Harry?" she quizzes like she already forgot they were talking about him.

"Your brother, Harry, about ants." Danny had more patience with Frannie than any other woman he'd ever known.

"Harry!" she exclaims.

"Do you know his number?"

"His phone number?"

"Am I not speaking clearly?"

"I don't know it!" How could she not know it? It used to be her number too! Where her memory has gone lately is another matter that can't be dealt with right now.

"You don't know your own brother's phone number?"

"Why can't you wait for the call here?" she is on to another subject.

"Because the church people only have this number. What's your brother's number?" he insists.

She puts the phone down and searches for her phone book while Danny stares at a moth jousting with the light bulb. She's back in a few seconds. "Harry's at 771-7128, but he's not there."

"Do you know where I can reach him?"

"You said it's about his ants," it occurs to her.

"Yeah, ants, where is he?"

"He's eating at that burger place."

"Oh, of course, I'll see you tomorrow."

"Okay Danny, and uh," she laughs as if someone told her a joke and she's about to pass it on. "Don't arise without me tonight, okay?"

"Smootcherooni!" he sings with a smile, turning his head to the left and right making sure no is within miles of earshot.

"Smootcheroni!" she is so sweet he hates to see her so taken with someone such as his dirty little self.

Ready to call Harry, he decides "first things first," drops a quarter in the phone and dials. It is July 5th, after all, and this is the night they promised to see each other a year ago.

"Hello," the scratchy diminutive voice answers.

"Can Mary Chu come to the phone?" he asks directly like he's trying to get someone paged off the assembly line.

"Mary Chu not here no more," the voice informs with no apology.

"Where is she?" Danny asks, while wondering if the little voice has a face that snickers when a man calls and wants to talk.

"We have Chin Tu," the voice answers.

"Thank you. Where is Mary?" Danny coaxes the man who doesn't realize what a shadow Danny is casting through the blotchy glass windows of the phone booth, a certain desperation clouding the periphery.

"No Mary here I say."

"You said that!"

"I know," and he hangs up on Danny.

Danny quietly struggles to regain his calm. An entire year and not a day had gone by without at least a sigh of anticipation and regret. Then he wonders for a moment if the Bible wasn't written to protect people from more than the reality of death.

Maybe it protects them from having to cope with love too.

Danny's Bible would absolutely contain at least a passage about the neurotic barricades which human nature jams in our way whenever we get the scent of a meaningful direction.

Mary Chu was simply the woman he had once wanted, in fact, selected, and all it required was to follow procedure and she'd have been his. That was years ago, but he still remembers choosing to talk the night away, and then became despondent for months after because given a chance to have extreme physical pleasure, he shied away.

Even when fulfillment is not elusive, some times we chase it away.

They were the original and more exotic version of Danny and Frannie. He was at once relieved to move on and disgusted for having given up on this woman who he both loved and detested.

He could never deny that he was as enticed as much as he was repelled by her background. He'd have to keep in touch forever, hoping for the off chance that he'd call when she could break away and meet him for one last dance in the cheap but tidy rental cottage.

Danny in his heart knew that he would never be up to the task of making love with Mary Chu, she being a professional and a sincere woman, simultaneously. It would be best if he never saw her again. But she was unfinished business and the only living evidence of his secret abundance of desire for passion.

Danny wanders over to unit number two and peers through the filthy windows. A heavy set man is sitting on the fiberglass desk chair, drinking cheap whiskey from a Burger King coffee cup. Danny remembers being caught sneaking a peak in the teenage girl's bedroom window in the house behind his when he was a kid. He's still excited and mortified by the memory.

He walks down the road to an all night truck stop and has a cup of coffee and a bag of taco chips while he reads the *Lucky Lotto Magic Number Guide*. Danny is proud that he's never purchased a lottery ticket. To him, winning the lottery is the most tragic form of success conceivable.

He invests the next two hours peering at the numbers, glancing through the window, waiting for Mary Chu to show up to finish things up.

Not more than two hours go by and you're at the phone booth picking him up. "Had to have some privacy," Danny explains. "Did anyone call?" You tell him the phones did not ring. He is silent after that.

You notice that he looks tired and withdrawn and you wonder if maybe he's been splashing cold water on his grimy face, giving himself that look – that exhausting look which you know so well – penetrating his own gaze in the cracked mirror of a Sunoco station restroom.

Only Zeke, Father Mulroy and you were there, not a single paying guest until Danny called for a ride back home. A while ago a young girl came in asking if you'd seen Mike Monroe, but you said "No, he hasn't been here tonight." "I assumed he'd be here," she chastised you. "Well, to tell you the truth, I never heard of him," you answered as she stomped out.

Like you don't have enough trouble without this! Your job used to be so pleasant and simple, finally a position that lets you capitalize on a talent you absolutely have. You aren't a writer, you're an editor and even if your name never gets printed, your corrections do.

But the cook book publishing business has become media conscious and suddenly anyone with a brand name can sell it to be attached to any discipline whatsoever.

So, here you were with Milton Mallet, the big talk show host, and he is putting the final touches on how his shirt is tucked in while your boss is telling you what an honor it will be to edit "A Minute Meal With Milton." Milton will not be writing or editing. You'll do the whole job. He will have his picture taken.

"If I'm writing and editing, what's he doing?" you asked.

"He's selling," your boss answered.

"Well, actually, my name and likeness will do the selling. I'll be playing golf," Milton smirked while talking to you through your boss. He never even made eye contact with you.

"I don't feel comfortable with this," you later told your boss. If you think I'm good enough to publish a book, I would hope you'd publish it under my name."

"You aren't Milton Mallet," he explained.

"He can't cook or write," you comment.

"The money's not in the writing, it's in the selling. When your name can sell a book, look me up. Until then, either do your job or someone else will. Writers are a dime a dozen," he made you cringe.

"What about creativity and originality?" you beseeched him.

"A dime a dozen." He turned his back and went back to tamping his pipe tobacco leaving you wondering if a minute with Milton might be more than one could bear.

At least your thoughts and ideas are appreciated at Danny's. Isn't that why people pick out certain places to hang out and certain friends to hang with? Isn't that why we believe in certain things, so that people will be attracted to us?

Damn it, you shouldn't have to be aggravated! You're so accustomed to not getting credit that you really don't need credit any more! You enjoy observing the human condition even if you don't share the symptoms!

Father Mulroy was a true specimen of hope for you. He had taken the big step toward becoming something and got annihilated for doing so. He's a perfect source of proof that accomplishment and achievement merely divert us from the real human experience.

"I saw myself as human bait, un-needing, un-giving, un-asking. Just a pure and thirsty mind sitting on the hook, waiting for the Lord to take a nibble and leave some truth behind on my barbs," he told you after you worked up the nerve to ask why he became a priest in the first place.

"Human bait, like God needs a lure, like God needs bright colors and wiggling tales to give you some attention?" you questioned him.

"And un-assuming," he added in response. "Un-assuming that there was a God, un-assuming that he would be aware of me or of the individual, so to speak," he explained. "You don't have to be responsible for your own actions! When you follow your instincts, they aren't your own actions at all!!" he said excitedly, a rare condition for the Father to be in.

"Even a child is known by his doings, Proverbs chapter 20, verse 11," you responded respectfully.

His cheek bones rose like a down and out drunken boxer who's been challenged to trade punches by a skinny teen out to prove himself to his scrawny girlfriend at the expense of the fighter's last grains of self-esteem.

"Love no false oath," he flung toward you like a sharp lance.

"Where is your church?" you asked, but there was no answer. "Love no false oath" he repeated as he blurred the fingerprints on the shot glass he'd been rotating.

"The secret of the Lord is with them that fear Him," you challenged.

He dropped his chin to his fists, stacked upon each other, resting on the round, damp "Miller Lite" coaster that boasts "It's It and That's That" in elaborate neon type.

"Surely the Lord is in this place, and I knew it not Genesis, chapter 28, verse 16, addressee unknown," he mumbled as he finished his shot of whiskey with a hoarse purr.

Danny walks in and immediately all attention returns to business, what's real being defined as what's in the cash register that wasn't there before he left on his mysterious trip to the telephone booth.

Chapter Sixteen

The phone rings. Danny doesn't want to talk to anybody. If this is Frannie, he might just dump her, right here and now, not because he doesn't love her but because he wants to break something that's important to him. Just to relieve the anxiety.

"Talk of the Town, we're closed," he mutters in to the black receiver.

"You didn't call," Father Pat mutters back.

"Father Pat?" he gasps.

"My ants didn't get here either," Father Pat laments.

"Did they call?" Danny comes to life.

"Yes. I spoke to a Bishop, very high in the organization," the Father reports.

"And?" Danny's eyes open wide as if he'll be hearing through them.

"And, before I forget, did you contact the ant person?" he asks.

"Harry?" Danny can not contain himself. "The Pope! What about the Pope!?" "Harry, of all people, getting in the way and he's not even involved!" Danny thinks to himself. He writes "Harry" in the dust on the bar mirror so he'll remember to ask Frannie to get them together.

"I purchased the ant farm but was told I must order the ants at another time," the Priest labors. "A mailing coupon will be with the farm," he continues.

"I'll get you together with Harry, my ant expert, when it gets there, now, please!" Danny is pivoting on his heels back and forth like he's on stage with the Four Tops.

"Here is what I was told."

Danny is panting like a slobbery Labrador chained to a stake watching an avalanche.

"Thou shalt not bring the hire of a whore, or the price of a dog, into the house of the Lord," the Priest recites.

"Yes?" Danny is waiting for the punch line.

"It means, preliminary, that, well, no," the Priest says honestly.

"No," Danny says as if to double-check the Priest's choice of words.

"Not that they don't seem interested. In fact, they seem quite taken with the idea. They called me several times to ask questions, then finally said they are completely not interested. It's not respectful, they said," concludes the Priest.

"The bums! Don't you see, they're stealing my idea!!! We've got to get directly to the big boss," Danny sputters.

"That may be out of my reach," the Priest apologizes.

"What is this, the White House, Red Square??? The Pope is, is – he's the Pope, for Christ's sake!!! Doesn't he rule on everything they do, not to mention life itself??" Danny is beside himself.

"I'm sure that the Pope is busy with other things. He is very restrained, you know," Father Pat explains.

"I see, like how restrained they were when they built the Vatican or when they decided the Pope would be dressed in 100 percent pure white silk and drink out of 2000 karat gold goblets, and of course, he sips on, what, orange Hi-C?"

"Yes, yes, but it is all in celebration of Jesus Christ. In the matter of the Pope, he remains, like us, simple servants of the Lord," concludes Father Pat.

"So I should sit around and wait for the second coming?"

"Unto them that look for Him shall He appear the second time, Hebrews, chapter 9, verse 28," the Priest responds.

"Don't give me that Bible double-talk. You know, the Bible is written in circles so no matter what you want it to say, it says. It says black and it says white at the same time. I'm trying to help pay your light bills!" Danny is losing is patience.

"I don't think it's going to fly," says the Father.

"When can I meet your ant friend?" he adds, hoping that the ant issue hasn't been killed off entirely because of the Vatican's lack of responsiveness.

"I'll get to Harry if you try to get to the Pope. Fair

deal?" Danny offers.

"The Pope for Harry. Okay," concludes Father Pat as he slips in to his usual state of mega-numbness.

Father Pat hangs up as he notices the postman coming around the sidewalk. What if he's carrying the Edmund Scientific carton?

"Harry," he thinks to himself.

"Boss!" a squeaky voice with husky overtones interrupts.

"Yes, Zero," he politely answers the disheveled small man.

"Lights are out again."

"I'm sorry," says the Father.

"You're sorry. You're sorry! You don't have to sleep here," says the short and bulky homeless man. They call him Zero because he's shaped like one.

"You don't need light to sleep, Zero," the Father answers calmly.

"We all appreciate the place to sleep, Father, but geeze, it's creepy in there with no light!"

Father Pat thinks about Danny, and decides that one must do what one must do. It's all for a good cause. More people rely on his church as a shelter for the night than for prayer on Sunday morning. "Pray to Jesus," he says to Zero.

"No offense, Boss, but Jesus is conveniently not around when it's bill paying time, ," Zero answers.

Father Pat doesn't want to hear any more about

it. "They said the lights will be back on tomorrow."

"Well, then, never mind, boss." Zero turns and returns to the sanctuary where everyone is settling down for a good night's sleep. The stained glass lets a bit of moonlight in and everyone senses that someone does care. Someone does notice their plight and will come to save them.

Chapter
Seventeen

Isadora was by far the most prominent new member of his family, and it seems certain to Harry that she will, at any moment, cave in to her reproductive nature.

She has been tunneling and burrowing for days, and just now Harry notices that she is quite nervous about something. The time has come. She must seal her fate.

"Good grief, what do you expect!?" Harry says out loud. "You're a fertile female, for goodness sake!" Harry is as tall and lanky as Isadora is long and clunky. He's a bit more unkempt than her, which she excuses for his lack of permanent employment.

Perhaps she is about to be taken by surprise. Nothing she does or thinks can make a bit of difference. "Accept your role and thrive within it," Harry advises.

Isadora's large head begins rising and rotating to an uncommonly severe degree, just to the brink of impossibility. Those nearby continue with their less regal activities.

Isadora's pincers open wide and they strike her wings and claw at them as her entire body rotates in jerky flinging motions.

And in seconds, she has ripped both her wings from her body, never to fly again, a sacrifice of deepest, darkest spiritual significance. "I commit to you for my lifetime." Her actions echo throughout the soils of her land. Not a single ant even pauses for a second as she makes this supreme pledge.

But they will serve her for the next 10 years as she propagates their world with fresh new recruits.

"Of course, you'll need a guy," Harry reminds her.

But given that she's fairly attractive, and is, after all, the only fertile female in the colony, she'll land some lucky fellow and create her very own civilization. Queen Isadora! For whom every lady will toil if she happens to be born without the ability to reproduce. The others can rip their wings off and have one big romp in the sack that will provide them with civilizations of their very own.

Harry can see the studs lining up, flexing their straight antennae, hoping to be the choices of royalty.

Harry can almost hear them, and he smiles because, after all these years, he's in on virtually every private ant joke. Queen Isadora looks over to some stud named Jake, likes what she sees, and beckons him to join her for a private moment.

He gives some high five's to one of his buddies, saunters up to her, his proud pelvis leading the way. She says "give me all you've got big boy," and Jake takes his best shot.

He backs away and says "Was it good for you?" and she answers dryly "Was what good for me?" and then he dies.

That's what he was there for. At least his purpose in life was clear and he didn't have to suffer through a lot of monotonous diversions until he achieved it.

"Are they aware of their own existence?" Harry wonders.

"I hereby crown you Queen Isadora, and proclaim that throughout the kingdom, all will devote their lives to you, never once asking why, laboring with the absolute faith that their loyalty will be rewarded appropriately when it should." Harry looks toward Isadora with respect. She is moved by the ceremony, although she seems a bit distracted by the big bead of sand which she feels deeply compelled to move.

She is so taken by the moment that she doesn't even sense the enormous disturbance which is about to occur as a stainless steel tweezers is guided through her skies, its tips flexing toward her and closing gently but securely on her leg, seizing her and lifting her in the air, a moment later, releasing her in a new land with 30 workers and an occasional yummy beetle or roach to serve at a celebratory state dinner.

"Hey, back the fuck off, asshole!!!" she glares up at Harry.

Harry smiles softly. He appreciates the order of things, the instant levels of command. The perfection of a living body of God's creatures instinctively doing the right thing. "I love you guys," he looks to

Jake who is already being carted off by his buddy who has suddenly committed himself to celibacy.

"You guys are what it's all about!" Harry proclaims.

Harry shouldn't be mistaken for a guy who is just silly about ants. He loves them, but he is consumed by why people do what they do too. Why they work at dumb jobs. Why they cheat on their wives. Why Frannie is attracted to that little goof ball, Danny. People are a great study and ants are just like them only more honest and direct.

He shudders at the idea of some sassy kid watching a line of ants swarm around an Oreo cookie he dropped on the sidewalk. The kid is at first taken by the military precision, the perfect order. Then he giggles and jumps up and down on them, killing as many ants as there are students in his school. And then his attention is diverted by some cute 15 year-old's blooming bosom and without a moment of regret or a chill for his sin, he strolls away leaving a virtual holocaust in his wake.

Harry understands his life because he understands their lives. Live, work, propagate, die. Ask nothing. Do what you need to. Your instincts are God. Follow them all.

"Maybe don't work too hard," he reminds himself.

Harry stumbled in to ant farming when he was just 12 years old. His Uncle Leon and Aunt Lenore had given him an Uncle Milton's Ant Farm for Christmas, and today he still remembers the bright green plastic sides, the clear plastic panels that would serve as a looking glass where he would study the perfect society.

However, there were no ants in the box, just a coupon:

TO ORDER YOUR LIVE ANTS, RETURN THIS COUPON TO OUR BREEDER TODAY.

Twelve year old Harry walked to the post office that evening and sent the coupon to the post office box in Little Rock, Arkansas.

A month later, the post man delivered his ants. About 30 of them, all looking just about identical except one larger ant which Harry immediately named Aunt Milton. Today you don't get a queen because it's illegal. Harry saves up queens in separate little breeding containers and he passes them on to friends who get caught up in the hobby.

Harry knows more about ants today than he does about people, but he is fairly certain that there are few differences and that if people followed their hearts instead of constantly trying to figure it all out, their lives would be more pleasant and more likely to fulfill whatever the Lord's wishes might be.

Harry doesn't think it matters what our purpose in life happens to be. He and Queen Isadora and her sister queens would accept their responsibilities and not question their limitations, and things will fall into place.

Harry could be considered gangly and frail, except he seems in fine health. A bit paler and his gait a bit more awkward and he'd fit nicely as one of those vegetarians who could really use a rare hamburger, just to give him some color.

He is surrounded by wood and glass ant farms, each with white note paper taped to its sides where he writes details on each civilization. It seems amazing that so many societies can live side by side without realizing the existence of the others.

"We only need to know what we find out without asking." Harry would suggest to his sister Frannie on many occasions when she would question why he is limiting his membership in society by dealing with nothing but his ants and the various derelicts he acquires on the streets.

"We only need to meet who we come across," he would add.

Oddly enough, as he is considering Frannie's simple-minded way of going about her life, he thinks that in a large sense, she conducts herself in complete agreement with his own attitudes.

Harry peers carefully in to colony 25, which he calls Rodeo Drive, after his favorite burger place, with its gaudy cowboy poster perched on the roof, luring the innocent, laughing at the more serious but failing pawn shops, hardware stores and the like on South High.

He looks for the little fellow with the red tip on his rear end.

"There you are, how's life treating you today Hester?" Harry speaks softly to the tiny worker, who for a reason not even clear to him is lugging a pebble through the labyrinth of tunnels seeming to have been constructed with no purpose at all to the community.

Hester pauses for a few seconds and looks through the clear glass wall which Harry keeps immaculately clean.

"Help me, Harry" he seems to gesture toward the heavy load behind him.

Harry marvels that Hester appears not to resent his lot in life at all, and he feels certain that this is appropriate.

Harry does not question his role in life at all either. He's not certain what that role is. But he is certain of what it isn't, as evidenced by the pile of classified ad pages strewn around the blue vinyl lounge chair plopped in the center of the ant room. Dozens of help wanted notices are vividly marked with big red X's.

"Not enough pay, too much responsibility, too irrelevant, too many hours, too few holidays," Harry would gleefully mutter as he'd mark them off each morning while sipping on his home squeezed grape-fruit juice.

"Public Relations Executive Wanted, no experi-ence required. Pleasant telephone voice and willing-ness to work long hours and succeed despite con-stant rejection," reads the one upon which he is underscoring his X, just to be sure he doesn't call it by mistake.

He calls very few of them. The last one was two weeks ago Tuesday.

"Public Interest Campaign Workers," the headline read.

"If you care about the people who have less than you, will you sacrifice making a lot of money to make a difference in their lives? No experience needed. Apply today. We pay full benefits and gener-ous commission."

"Hello, I am calling about the campaign job you advertised in *The Blade* this morning," Harry spoke pleasantly and distinctly, giving every letter its full due. Harry felt that even the letters of a word de-served to be fully expressed considering that their entire course of events concludes after having been uttered by him. Harry felt sorry for words and ideas once they were conveyed.

"I'll connect you to our sales department," the youthful voice responded.

"Sales, Irv," the quick and stout man answered.

"I'm calling about the job." Harry was brief and to the point.

"Yes, do you have any experience?" Irv also liked to be brief.

"The ad says I don't need any," Harry responded.

"Yeah. But do you have any?" Irv retorted.

"What kind would be applicable?" Harry asked.

"Selling things to old people would be good," Irv answered.

"What would I be selling?" Harry isn't opposed to selling as long as it sells itself.

"Good government," Irv cackled.

"What is there to sell?" Harry was puzzled.

"You'd be selling participation in the State Public Interest Campaign. We solicit signatures and donations to help us prod the legislators into doing their jobs more responsively to what's good for the public," he explained.

"Why do they have to give you money for that?" Harry asked.

"Cause we like to eat," Irv was getting impatient.

"What do they get for their donations?" Harry wanted to know.

"They get more people collecting other donations," he concluded.

"Then if everything just stopped, nothing would change?" Harry surmised.

"You have the wrong attitude, young man," and

Irv hung up.

Harry looks at Hester and then glances toward Queen Isadora who is at that moment conducting a meeting of her own with her new workers and slaves. "Now, about sex –" she mutters, and all the eligible males take off like jack rabbits.

Somehow even the ants can tell that Harry is confused, but not to the extent that he'll alter his day's plans. That pile of x'd out newspapers tells them that he has simply not been given his instructions, that somehow his talents and abilities are brewing and that sooner or later, his lot in life will be determined and he'll suddenly find himself doing it.

The doorbell rings and Harry just says "Come in," without looking toward the door, his attentions fully absorbed as he marvels at the lack of interaction between the newly coronated Queen and the rest of the civilizations surrounding his apartment.

"Why don't you fill these things with water and get some fish?" Danny takes the entire murky room in with a quick glance. "At least get some color."

"Hi Danny," Harry greets him, still without looking toward him.

"Here. I bought you something, for you and your pals." Danny is smiling devilishly as he hands Harry a brown paper bag.

"Thank you." And Harry just sets the bag down.

"Open it!" Danny instructs.

Harry opens the bag and pulls out a pickle jar. Danny gestures to open it and Harry obeys.

"They were in the bar. I saved their lives," Danny explains as Harry stares at three ants sitting at the bottom of the smelly jar.

"That was kind of you, Danny." Harry smiles toward him.

"What were they doing when you found them?" he asks.

"They were playing pinochle," Danny tiring of the ant subject.

"They're probably males. Too bad," Harry sighs.

"What's wrong with being males?" Danny asks.

"They're going to die. They probably just mated," Harry explains.

"Oh yeah, well you know why male ants die before their female ant girlfriends?" Danny kids.

"No, why?" Harry asks.

"Because they want to!!!!" and he chortles. Harry is not moved.

"They are God's creatures just like you and me and their lives are significant." Harry is very serious about his ants.

"Ants is ants," says Danny.

"There are over 2000 different kinds of ants, Harry. Ants ain't ants," Harry mimics Danny's style.

"Yeah, well, that's why I'm here Harry. Your sister said you were at that burger place but when I went there they said you were at home, and of course, no one seems to have any idea how to reach you. Do you have a phone here or not?" Danny asks.

"I forgot to pay the bill when they were printing the phone book so they left me out. It didn't matter. If you need me, you can find me," Harry rationalizes.

"I need to ask you about the ants so I can tell this old Priest who is going to sell my embroidery items to the Vatican." Danny makes it seem very simple.

"Oh," says Harry nonchalantly, "Well, what do you want to know?" he offers.

Danny can't figure out a thing he wants to know. He can't imagine anyone wanting to know anything about ants.

"I'm going to bring him here, is that okay with you?" Danny asks.

Harry is wandering around the ant colonies and is watching the activity in one home very carefully. The question seems to escape him.

"This one right here is all females and a few cows. I'll have to tend to them," Harry casually explains.

"How about the Priest, Harry?" Danny reminds him.

"Sure, bring him any time," he answers.

"They raise cows in there?" Danny asks. "Moooo," he comments to the females and cows.

"Actually, they capture and enslave aphids, and

they milk them for food. It's a real treat," Harry explains.

"Aphid juice, great, well Harry –" Danny turns to address all of the ants too "– and of course, your family here, I'll be seeing you. I'll give you a call about the Priest."

"Okay, well have a good day Danny." Harry bids him farewell, and just as Danny is about to leave, he adds "Know of any job that might be up my alley, Danny?" Harry asks so Danny will tell Frannie that her brother is industrious.

"Harry, I think it would be best if you focused on your sanity a bit first. You've got a big heart. The ants love you. The bums love you. A little involvement with the real world would look good on your resume," Danny advises him and dashes out the door.

"Wait, how's Frannie?" Harry calls Danny back.

"She's fine."

"Her head's been aching, she tells me," Harry seems concerned.

"She's just thinking too much, nothing to worry about there," Danny suggests, although he too is hoping that by ignoring her complaints, they'll go away quietly.

Harry shrugs off the entire matter, grabs his portable tape recorder and follows Danny out. He's hoping that some ants will have found the marshmallow he left on the back porch and that enough will be there to make some noises his Sennheiser microphone can pick up.

He smiles as he anticipates breaking their language code sooner or later.

Chapter Eighteen

Frannie is dreamy. She and Father Mulroy are mistress and master of the house of Danny. They are baby-sitting the Talk of the Town, like grandparents passing time while the child sleeps until the parents have had their weekly chance to pretend they are still relevant members of the party set.

Frannie is wrapping the bright yellow thread from one of his embroidery spools around her finger. Father Mulroy is reading a paperback which Danny had insisted he read. It's called *Multi-Level Marketing: Tomorrow's Pyramid of Success*.

Zeke and you are at Tobo Arena, surrounded by a society which finds reality boring and doesn't mind substituting dramatized reality as a more valid place to be entertained.

You are sure that if you were viewing these 10,000 crazy fools from above, you would stand out like a sore thumb.

But none of them seem to notice or take exception to your presence. "You ever see guys like me here?" you ask the sad, bulky, nicotine-stained eyeballs lodged in a soft, hefty, beer keg of a man sitting next to you.

"A guy like you in a place like this?" he gives you this real dumb look, closing his ample eyelids over his puffy, inflated eyes.

"Yeah, you know." And you're rolling your hand like a water wheel to emphasize the unspoken, that you are an exception to this detestable crowd of misbegotten sons and daughters.

"I never seen you here." You feel immediately relieved until he continues, "But I seen your old lady sucking off the boys in the can!!!" he laughs uproariously and smacks his beer against his friends, suds pouring all over their laps.

"Want some?" he asks as he points to the puddle setting on the ample cliff separating his belly from his chest.

You look to Danny who says, "These are the people, Al. Relate to them and you go to heaven."

You think somewhat to the contrary, but suddenly you can't hear yourself think because the entire crowd is on their feet and some goof called "Adolph the Purifier" enters the arena to some hideous German march. He is of course tossing out souvenir swastika medals to the eager young kids in the audience. The fathers and mothers are swearing at him. He goose-steps into the ring and is pummeled by beer cups.

Then you hear the mighty sounds of our national anthem and everyone seems genuinely joyous about having been born on this particular soil.

"Mighty Joe Young" the tuxedoed announcer barks at the crowd and you can imagine that the joker who is firing down the aisles toward the ring was just bazookaed out of a Super Hero comic book.

Looking around you again, you're sure everyone here has read that particular book over and over again.

"This is the finest entertainment in existence," Danny proudly hails. Zeke nods in complete agreement. "I share that view entirely." His head wiggles as he renders his commitment to that point.

"These guys are probably roommates," you whisper to Danny. "They're like Fred Astaire and Ginger Rogers, every step measured to the second, don't you know that?" you ask.

"Tell that to him," Danny suggests as he points to the man-mountain next to you, still soaking from the beer you so rudely refused. He's standing on top of his chair screaming "Death Claw, Death Claw, Death Claw, Death Claw." Popcorn is careening out of his mouth and landing unnoticed on all the big hair surrounding him.

"And now, for the heavyweight championship of the world!" the announcer begins.

He continues that the Nazi is presently the champion, undefeated Mighty Joe the challenger.

On closer inspection, you realize that the Nazi is clearly Hispanic, or a very large Filipino. "This guy isn't even German!" you tell Danny.

"You're not supposed to study them!" Danny groans. "Just accept things for how they appear and you'll be a lot happier," he adds.

"You do understand that this is complete non-sense, don't you?" you are cautious to say.

"This is not nonsense. This is more real than a baseball game. It's more serious than brain surgery. It's more dangerous than pancreatic cancer." He is livid with you.

"But it's fake!" you declare as the two wrestlers have ignored the bell and have already thrown the referee over the ropes and he is bleeding from both ears on the ring apron. The Nazi is trying to remove one of the eyes of the pretty American hero, and the hero is writhing in agony from having been bitten in the neck by the Nazi's black leather wrapped girl-friend manager.

"The people like it. It gets them excited. Are they genuinely excited or not?" he asks.

You look around. "They are excited but they've been misled. If they knew the truth, they wouldn't possibly be excited," you calmly explain.

"They came for excitement, not to analyze how they got that way!" he concludes. "This is not fake. They are feeling real things. That's why it works. That's the wave of the future. Someday they'll play baseball and football this way." He looks back to the ring where the Nazi is displaying his clawed hand to the crowd, chasing after it in the air like it has a mind of its own. The American is on the floor and seems to be dead except that every now and then his leg twitches.

"Death Claw, Death Claw, Death Claw!" the entire crowd is screaming.

And the Nazi chases his claw directly in to the American's stomach, the American now in a complete spasm as if he just got electrocuted. The referee tries to toss the Nazi to the side but he slams his other clawed hand over the referee's skull, and the referee joins the American in his spasm.

Suddenly, the Nazi's mistress enters the ring carrying a baseball bat. She plants a kiss on the American, pulls an American flag out of her enormous cleavage, and beats the devil out of her Nazi boyfriend until he is pinned by the American, the referee coming back to consciousness just long enough to whack his hand against the canvas three times.

The speakers roar with "God Bless America" and a big Asian woman a few rows ahead of you starts belting out the lyrics like she's Ethel Merman.

"Say what you want, but go to a baseball game – go to the World Series, the Superbowl, anything you want anywhere and not one other entertainment or sport can measure up to this. You come here for excitement and you get it. Wrestling is the most honest sport in the world. End of story," Danny explains to you and Zeke. Zeke continues to sway his head to the beat of Danny's every word. And you can't deny the truth of what he's saying either.

It might kill your recipe book editing career, but you're going to stick close to this guy. Danny is in the backseat of life driving a very hard bargain.

Chapter Nineteen

Frannie at this moment is trying to shrug off that damned headache as she stands somberly behind the cash register at Talk of the Town. Father Mulroy notices that she looks a bit pale, but he attributes it to spending an excess amount of time with Danny.

"Are you all right?" Father Mulroy asks.

"Just my darned migraine again," she winces.

"Dear girl, you should go home and rest," he suggests.

"Danny would kill me," she answers.

"We are not doing something holy here. I'm sure he'd understand," the Father replies.

"You tell Danny that this isn't holy," she says.

"I would tell him that you have to take care of your health. What does your doctor say about these headaches?" he asks.

"I just have to live with them, I guess," she answers.

"It seems like an unnecessary struggle in this day and age," he notes.

"My horoscope says I'm supposed to be struggling as long as Saturn is around," she tells him as she presses her thumbs against her temples and rubs the pain.

"It's been around forever," she adds.

"Saturn is just a state of mind," the Father suggests.

"Yeah, a state of exhaustion," Frannie confides.

She won't go home before closing time because Danny would be disappointed in her. On the other hand, this headache cannot be ignored even while she focuses on the rhododendron bush which has been blooming for two straight months in the clay pot by the window. She's been tending to it daily and knows that its success is a sign that something is about to burst.

Chapter Twenty

Danny can't help himself. He is drawn to the church. The door squeals open and a cloud of dust fills the air. St. Matt's is the kind of place where this much dust could collect in a single day.

A nun walks out just as Danny is entering.

"Do you guys spray this stuff here?" he asks as he tries to whisk it all away with his waving hands.

She looks toward him and glares "These are the things of man. Ours are the affairs of the Lord." Then she sneezes. Danny laughs as he continues through the sorry door and saunters into the dim chapel.

Out of nowhere, a hand grips his and shakes it firmly.

"Welcome to St. Matt's. You're a friend here, so don't be afraid to cry," an apparently elderly, but probably 40ish, short and heavyset homeless man greets him.

Danny wonders how he got so large considering his obviously limited economic status.

Danny says "I'm fine, really" and looks around to see several dozen shabbily dressed street people just sort of hanging out. One is reading a skin magazine and not even noticing the pictures. A lady is counting Good n Plenty's as she returns them from her hand to the box. A much older woman is unraveling her old woolen scarf.

"Is there a service going on here or what?" Danny

asks the round, convivial man.

"Nope. Just us. I'm Zero." Danny says "No kidding."

"Yep, Zero. That about sums it up, I'm sorry to say," he adds as Danny is staring at the guy's ample nose. Zero has the largest nostrils Danny has ever seen. He can't imagine a person needing as much air as these would provide.

"Nothing. Nada," Zero continues as he opens his clenched hands and drops nothing to the ground. "Nothing in my hands, nothing up my sleeves!" he seems to have come to terms with his situation.

"All of you the same?" Danny scans the ragged group of people who, despite their lot in life, appear to be rising above it all.

"Hey you, Pinkie, you got anything?" he bellows over to the lady who is experimenting with bubble gum to see how long it will stay stretched between her two thumbs as she pokes holes in it with her tongue.

"I got another half a stick of gum, you want it?" she offers kindly.

"You, Half-Pint, do you have any personal belongings of any kind?" Zero asks the sleeping dwarf on the pew behind him.

The thickly bearded four footer grunts and awakens just enough to answer "I got my teeth" and he shows them. "My bottom ones anyway!" and he smiles, then falls back asleep.

"None of us has got anything," Zero proclaims.

"We got Jesus!" you hear Pinkie remind him.

"And he's coming back to save us," Zero reminds Danny.

"Well, say hello for me." Danny smiles and walks away following the path to Father Pat's study. This time his feet walk smaller than before. And they're kind of dull.

"What's an ant farm with no ants?" Father Pat is murmuring as he assembles his Uncle Milton Ant Farm on the shelf next to his lectern. He's comparing the picture in the catalog to the actual product to make sure no parts are missing.

"No ants in the ant farm, huh Father?" Danny enters the room and the Priest hardly bats an eye.

"Gotta send for them," he's disappointed.

"But your idea is doing much better," he adds. Danny's face springs to life. He sits down.

"Did they change their minds?" Danny speaks in Father Pat's face, trying to divert his attention from the empty ant farm.

"I can be anywhere at anytime to meet with them!" he adds.

"You won't have to lift a finger, apparently," and Father Pat motions Danny toward the newspaper folded on the old desk, already collecting dust. Danny's eyelids are jittering and pulling so tightly, the

Father can see the outline of Danny's pupils embossing themselves in his skin.

"What is this?" asks Danny as he picks up the paper.

"A wish come true. They're doing your idea. I can't believe it, but they will actually be selling Pope T-Shirts. Congratulations."

Danny reads the headline on the business page.

POPE TO BECOME LATEST
NAME BRAND

The Vatican today announced through its agent, Kathy A. Kelly Artists Representatives, that it is proceeding with a world-wide licensing program which will permit select companies to produce merchandise bearing the likeness of the Pope. The licensed firms will then be permitted to market such products wherever the Pope appears.

"We estimate that revenues of approximately $1.3 billion can be generated by this project," explained Bishop Heaton Hutt, who has fiduciary responsibility to the Vatican for North American activities. "The success of this effort will combine with our recent turnaround in local collections to make the Church financially vibrant," he concluded.

At the same time, the Vatican has registered the name "Pope" and the likeness of the current

Pontiff as registered service marks of the Vatican, and has concluded arrangements with several major novelty manufacturers to begin product development.

Asked if this effort tarnishes the image of the Church as a non-commercial enterprise, Bishop Hutt commented that "It gives good people a chance to choose something other than rock stars as the images which define them."

Danny is emotionally augering into the creaky floor.

"I've been screwed by the Pope," is all he can mutter.

"Screwed by the Pope." And he walks out, mouth drooping to the floor, newspaper headline falling slowly to the dusty ground.

He gazes at the photograph, a bathroom microphone made out of soap, the cutline reading: *Pope on a Rope, Does It Have A Prayer?*

The Priest digs deep in to his memory, closes his eyes and declares, "Though He was rich, yet for your sakes He became poor, that ye through His poverty might be rich."

Danny shakes it off and locks his vision on the eyes of the confused Priest. "Yeah, yeah, well deliver this to the head banker: Danny DeMarco is not going to roll over and play dead. Someone wants to start playing God with me, I've got a special little passage you can read to them.

"And what is that, Danny?" the Priest asks meekly.

"It goes like this. Eat my socks."

With a promise to speak again after things settle down, Danny leaves the Priest to privately lament his missing ants, and Danny is heading for the exit, passing through the dark chapel.

"Been to confession?" Zero is back at Danny's side asking questions.

"Been to the well and come back empty," Danny confesses.

"Sorry to hear that. We've all been to that well before, haven't we?" Zero asks everyone.

"Had a couple of drinks from it, myself," Pinky lifts her gum wad toward him and toasts Danny's future happiness.

Half-Pint wakes up and blurts, "There's always hope."

Zero adds brightly, "There's always Jesus."

"Here and gone," says Danny.

"But he'll be back any day now," Pinky reminds him.

"Well, maybe I can sell the T-Shirts for that," Danny comments sadly.

"I'd like a nice Jesus blanket," a heavy-set guy way up front stands up and places his order. "I believe in Jesus Christ, don't get me wrong," he reminds everyone.

"Do you really believe that Jesus will return?" Danny asks the group?

"Of course," says Zero.

"That hope is all we've got," chimes Pinky.

"Jesus will return and the believers will be saved," Half-Pint struggles to recite, then conks out once again.

"How will you know when he gets here?" Danny asks Zero.

"Mr. DeMarco. When Jesus Christ returns he will make himself known. And he will settle all records," the booming voice roars from the rear of the chapel. Father Pat walks with a tall wooden cane toward the group.

"Miracles!" exclaims a voice from way up front. "Locusts" says another.

"It's our shot," says Zero, softly.

"I'll have a home and my children will come back to me. I'll work for a living and we won't spend all of our money, but we'll spend most of it!" he laughs, enjoying the magical spell he has woven.

"Father, seriously, when the Messiah returns how will we recognize him? What will he look like?" Danny is truly curious. "How do you know it's not me?"

"It couldn't be you. I'm sure of that," the Priest smiles gently.

"There'd be miracles," he laughs.

"But I'm due, that's for sure," adds Danny.

"Some say the world as we know it will end; some say the world as we know it will just begin!" Father Pat explains.

"I'll know him when I see him," grunts Half Pint, now awakened from his stupor and all ears to the conversation.

"Perhaps you will, Half Pint," remarks Father Pat.

"Thousands of years ago, it was believed that there would always be 36 people on earth who, unknown to them, are the eyes and ears of the Messiah's return. All 36 of them will know He is here when He arrives and they will find Him," Father Pat explains.

"Hey, maybe we're them!" exclaims Zero.

"That's why we don't have anything else to do!" Pinkie concludes.

"Yeah, we're here to wait," says Pinkie. "So don't give me a hard time!" she laughs toward Danny and Father Pat.

"I've gotta go," Danny says.

"Take me to your ant person," Father Pat reminds him.

"Call me when your ants get here and he'll come train them for you," Danny answers.

"Join us again sometime," says Zero.

"I just might," answers Danny on his way up the aisle to leave, his brain whirring like a gyroscope.

"Failure is the mother of opportunity," Danny remembers reading from the audio success book he listens to when he drives around by himself.

As he walks, Danny counts the homeless like a flight attendant making sure no one has snuck on board pretending to see some old aunt off to Dubuque.

"We'll let you know if we spot him," giggles Pinky.

"Spot who?" asks Zero.

"Our Savior!" drawls Half-pint.

"He must be running late!!" adds Pinky who then pops a big bubble that echoes throughout the tired old church.

Bishop Paul Flagg hails from Toronto, Ontario, where he was seldom seen in church or Bible school during his early childhood. Raised in a small apartment near Yonge and Wellesley, he was too well off to suffer from the despair that might have made him a religious child.

If it hadn't been for the tragic traffic accident which killed his mother and father when he was 10, he probably would have continued on his merry way toward becoming an auditor or something that would draw on his mathematic prowess.

But when his Aunt Anita took him under her wing after the accident, religion became an important part of his life. Oddly, the woman was completely ignorant of the Bible and the tenents of her own religion. But she was so pious, her platitudes formed their own sort of Bible and young Paul Flagg became a disciple of her own sort of religion.

"Did you know that before Jesus was crucified, He refused to eat even a forkful of the last supper?" she would toss little inventions to Paul, the captive student. "How do you know that, Aunti?" he would constantly question the source of her knowledge.

"And the Lord commanded, let no child question his Auntie's teachings" she raised her hands to the heavens and continued "Dear Lord, give this young man the balance to survive his trip through hell," she prayed. Auntie Anita believed that after death, a person's spirit went to heaven via hell. "Everyone goes to hell and those that lived a good life just wave hello on their way to heaven," she would explain.

"To the victors go the spoils!" she would shout, the "spoils" being a free ride through hell just for the sake of gloating.

Paul entered the seminary when he was 19. He immediately adopted all of the Catholic Church's teachings as absolute truth because they were easier truths than those taught by the Church of Auntie Anita. He was grateful for having been saved from her grasp and he pledged to never sway.

He resented anyone who questioned anything they were taught. "We are here to learn the Bible, not to question it. We are here to study the interpretations, not to interpret them," he interrupted another of the many annoying late-night debates among his bright fellow students.

They called him "Half-Mast." "You always seem to be mourning your own life, Flagg," his roommates would constantly remind him of his incessant dreariness. "Perhaps your mourning is not a bit premature!" they laughed.

"Fools despise wisdom and instruction," he countered with another of his ceaseless Bible quotes.

"He that walketh with wise men shall be wise, but a companion of fools shall be destroyed," he continued.

"We should serve in newness of spirit, and not in the oldness of the letter," argued Flagg's nemesis, Terry Mulroy, the young tiger, easily the most robust of the small class.

"Pray everywhere, lifting up holy hands, without wrath and doubting!" Flagg screeched.

"Go and cry unto the gods which ye have chosen; let them deliver you!" Mulroy quoted from the Book of Judgments.

"You doubt who you are praying to?" Flagg was startled by the feisty Mulroy.

"God would respect a healthy skepticism," Mulroy responded.

"I mourn the precious hours you could devote to prayer instead of wasting them on doubt," Flagg answered solemnly and the conversation ended until the next time.

The final performance was conducted years later after Flagg's stridency provided him with great success climbing up the Church's ladder. A direct by-product of that success would be Terry Mulroy's failure. It was a simple ceremony. Mulroy, preaching to his small flock of itinerants, made a simple suggestion to help them through their difficult times:

"Jesus Christ could be here with you today. As He was 2000 years ago. And who is to know that He isn't? Who is to know that the man or woman standing next to you at this very moment is not Jesus?"

Mulroy suggested solemnly, but with that smile which everyone grew to trust.

"My friends, Jesus Christ was no different than you or me. We are the ones with the power. We created Jesus. We can create our own second chances. Our own second lives. If Jesus Christ did nothing our church teaches us, if Mary was just a happy housewife whose husband insisted on a private life so you couldn't tell that she even had a husband, and if Jesus performed not a single miracle except having brought some simple wisdom in to a complicated time, we would still have created Him. And we can create your next life too." Mulroy was as enchanted with these thoughts as was his audience.

"God gave us the ability to create new truths that make our life more tolerable. The difference between happy and successful people and those who live lives of misery is what kind of truths each was able to concoct for themselves. You can be happy if you choose to be. You can rise above your own rags and poverty if you choose to. And if you doubt that, look to the Bible. Look to the church. Look to Jesus Christ, because He is our invention too. Jesus is each and every one of us at some moment in our lifetimes!"

This event was later reported to Bishop Flagg. It was the last sermon ever performed by Terry Mulroy under the auspices of the Catholic Church.

Autumn in New York City, if one could perform a karma-scan, everything would be a perfect blue. The air is like a skin connecting every person in the enormous crowd which has politely gathered along Fifth Avenue. Fake velour stanchions segregate the pseudo-aristocrats in front of Trump Tower from the riff-raff. The camera catches one of the women wearing a leather skirt so tight, the T-bar line from her exciting panties is embossed in the red animal skin. The top of her stockings is revealed as she reaches over to the souvenir cart and inspects a pair of sunglasses with Holy Crosses emblazoned on each lens.

Realizing that these are not authorized souvenirs when she notices that the catchy Pope caricature is missing, she scoffs at the vendor and drops the glasses in his cart.

Very comical, but you are more concerned with the Pontiff himself. If he looked like Andy Griffith, would he have ever made it this far? Did this gentle but stirring demeanor come from years of practice in front of the shaving mirror? Could he possibly be a natural, all of this attention feeling unwarranted and mysterious to him?

There he goes, in his bullet-proof Plexiglas cage erupting out of the back of the white Mercedes limousine. You can imagine Jerry Lewis singing "You'll Never Walk Alone" while a giant hand comes down and shakes the glass box until sparkles float all around inside it, the Pontiff never altering his expression, always the calm believer.

"They love him everywhere he goes," says the TV announcer from his vantage point high above Times Square where he is surrounded by little reminders of things the show's sponsors would appreciate if we purchase immediately.

"Well, the Church has made sure they can all keep a little bit of him as a souvenir," adds his bubbly male companion. They had wanted a female, but the Pope's special services squadron of advance men felt it was inappropriate.

"Tomorrow he'll be in Detroit, and we expect more of the same. There's a genuine love of the Pope everywhere he goes," the announcer exclaims.

"You ain't whistling Dixie," the companion adds.

The camera zooms in on vendors hawking all sorts of official Pope Paraphernalia, and your stomach sinks.

"Why didn't you tell me?" you ask Danny the next morning.

"Tell you what?" asks Danny, screaming from the back room of Talk of the Town, all sorts of noise coming from the machinery, so loud you can hardly hear.

"They took your idea," you yell back, looking around the corner you see the small man snipping off the red thread from a white piece of fabric. Danny is so totally focused on the task, he doesn't seem to notice that you've arrived.

At his side, zipping back and forth carrying boxes of merchandise out to the bar are three aromatically incorrect fellows, one older and heavyset, another quite possibly a woman, but you can't be certain because she has perhaps a dozen layers of clothing covering her tiny frame.

"Who are these people?" you ask.

"God's children," answers Danny.

"And we're busy," says Zero.

"God's work," adds Pinky, her tongue blasting through her wad of gum to punctuate her commitment.

"Must be done," blurts Half-pint, his goldfish eyeballs and his little body bobbing and floating like he's been injected with time-release ether.

"We're just getting in on the periphery to fund the main attraction," explains Danny.

"Motown, brother," says Zero.

"Today Detroit, Tomorrow Toledo!" professes Pinky.

"Why do you think they call it holy?!!!" laughs Half-Pint.

"Holy Toledo!!!!" Zero chortles.

They are surrounded by hundreds of shirts, aprons, every kind of wearable item you can imag-

ine, all featuring the "Pope." Pope World Tour. Pope
in the Poconos. Pope this, Pope that, lots of sparkles
and --

There is a heavy banging on the door.

It must be Zeke, too early again.

No, it's a policeman standing impatiently with
three men in black. Priest garb. There is a big
pickup truck behind them.

"Can I help you?" you ask through the window
screen.

"We have a warrant," says the policeman.

The Priests look at you with utter disgust. You
hope they don't think the smell is coming from you.

Danny comes charging out of the back room, carrying a brown box of Pope goods. "A warrant for
what?" he asks.

The policeman walks in, followed by the Priests
who continue looking at you in a way that makes
you feel guilty and pitiful.

"You're a thief," says the first Priest.

"From the Church," adds the second.

The third reaches in to Danny's brown box and
pulls out a "I Partied with the Pope" headband. He
holds it out with two fingers as if it was a dead fish.

"This is counterfeit," he reads his verdict to the
policeman.

"I have to confiscate all of this," he apologizes to
Danny as Half-pint walks by them and casually uri-

nates on the sidewalk. Two of the Priests watch the puddle of liquid begin seeping toward their feet, but in the name of solemnity, they don't move.

"Just you wait a minute, this is a free world, and the Pope belongs to everyone and –" says Danny before he is interrupted by the first Priest.

"But we own his image. It's a registered trademark. Like Gucci."

"It's all contraband now, gotta take it all away," says the Policeman as he signals the men from the truck to come in and do their thing.

A half hour later, it's all gone, including the embroidery machine.

Danny is sitting behind the bar. He's been stone faced throughout the entire ordeal.

"It was a diversion. They did exactly what I had hoped for," Danny reaches under the bar and pulls out a folded white sweatshirt.

"I want them to think they own the whole shebang, so they'll be nice little content Priests and not pester taking it the next logical step," he explains.

"What's the next step, Danny?" you ask cautiously.

Danny dramatically holds out the glowing red, blue and white sweatshirt with lots of sparkles in the letters that read:

The Second Coming
July 5 Toledo Ohio

"All of the miracles, live and in person," croons Danny.

"But Jesus is theirs too," whines Pinky.

"Jesus is ours," comes the voice of Father Mulroy who has been watching this strange event unfold. "Is Jesus not in your heart?" he asks.

"He's in my heart, that's for sure!" says Zero.

"Is Jesus not in your soul?" the Father asks Pinky.

"Jesus is my soul!" she answers.

"Then you and Jesus are inseparable. Anyone who claims Jesus must also claim you," Father Mulroy concludes.

"Nobody'd want to claim you!" laughs Zero as he points to Half-Pint.

"Well, then, let's get on with it," says Danny, and although no one is quite sure what he is referring to, he seems to have a plan and nobody in attendance has anything more serious to attend to.

"Get on with what?" you ask from behind Father Mulroy.

"The Pope's the Pope. My friends here believe that Jesus is returning and I'm going to help them find him." Danny puts his arms around Zero and Pinky. Half Pint feels neglected but Danny gestures for him to join them, and they form one happy if odd family.

"You're going to find Jesus?" you ask. "Are we talking about becoming re-born?"

"I'm talking about shaking his hand and getting him out in the streets, giving him some access to modern communications, giving him some proper management," Danny explains as Zero, Pinky and Half-Pint look suitably confused but proud to be part of whatever's going on.

"First, we've got to find him. The Father here says he could be anyone. We've got to cull that down a bit," Danny beams.

"You really think that Jesus has returned, that the Second Coming has arrived?" you gasp incredulously.

"Why not?" says Mulroy. "Maybe he never left. Maybe he passes among us," he speculates.

"Who's to say he isn't you, Al!" Danny points to your forehead. "Who's to say?" he repeats and everyone lowers their heads and you fear they are praying that it's not true.

"Maybe it's Zeke," you suggest to take the pressure off. Father Mulroy and Danny look at each other to consider the possibility.

"Could be," says Mulroy.

"I have serious doubts," says Danny, and they both laugh. You're glad Zeke hasn't caught wind of this yet. He'd be very confused, you're sure.

Chapter
Twenty Three

"I never imagined you could be so religious, Danny." Frannie comments as they walk along the beach. From behind, it looks like she's holding hands with a large walking pear.

Frannie and Danny, a couple of pals on the Lake Erie shore, just to the east of the now shut-down Harborfront, a charming invention that should have worked.

Danny had been feeling guilty for having spent so much time with the church group over these past few weeks.

"My boy, trying to find Jesus," she sighs adoringly.

"The people seem to think he's coming, so who am I to begrudge them their Lord?" Danny explains. "Personally, I don't know, but every night we go looking for him."

"Where do you look, Danny?" she asks.

"At the kind of places he'd go. You know, the library, ice cream parlors, hardware stores."

"Do you think he'd know who he is?" she holds him closely. You are walking along side them, wondering the very same things although you feel out of your element plodding through the sand in your chukka boots.

"He wouldn't know. It'll be a complete surprise to him," Danny explains.

"How's your head been?" Danny asks Frannie.

"It gets better and worse, but the other day it was

really bad. I saw a bus stop just short of a little boy reaching for his ball in the street, and, well, my head started hurting and I couldn't catch my breath either," she explains.

"Have you talked to the doctor?" you ask.

"He says I have to learn to live with the headache," she says.

"What about this breathing thing?" Danny is concerned.

"I guess I was just scared," she answers.

"Well, have you checked your horoscope lately?" Danny tries to lighten things up.

"What sign are you again?" you ask.

"Aquarius!" she exclaims. "With severe Saturn influences!"

"This is the dawning of the age of Aquarius, age of Aquarius," you sing until Danny looks at you and says "Can it!"

"It said yesterday that I have to stick with my pressures and be supportive of my friends even if it causes me grief," she explains.

You feel like an intruder. Danny probably invited you 'cause of last night, you think. You remember wincing when Danny asked if you would mind mopping up when they closed.

You were becoming maybe a bit too familiar to him. And unlike Zeke, you were still a paying customer.

"Mop?" you asked.

"Yeah, the floors," Danny answered glibly, like you've been doing this for years. By day, the customer. By night, the janitor.

"I don't work for you," you responded.

"Keep this up and you never will. There's opportunity on the horizon," he reprimanded you.

So, you mopped the place up, which only took a few minutes because there hadn't been more than half a dozen customers all night long.

The only customer of significance this evening was that roly-poly guy who seemed unlikely to be able to pay for his own drink, let alone Zeke's.

"Hey, have a seat, hate to see a fellow drink by himself," Zeke offered to the man.

"So, what brings you here tonight?" Zeke started out.

"Jesus," he answered quickly.

"I'm looking for Jesus along with Mr. Danny. Is he here?" Zero asked.

"Danny is not here, but tell me about Jesus," Zeke continues.

"Would you care for another drink?" you approached them both.

"Well, I sure would, except that I gave it up," Zero smiled at you.

"Well, how about your friend?" you asked him by rote.

"He should probably give it up too," the character

smiled.

You couldn't help but agree. He obviously had seen through your charade, so you sat down on a stool after buying and then pouring a brew for yourself.

"First time here?" Zeke asked the charming Zero.

"I beg your pardon, boss?" Zero is offended.

"He's been here a lot, after hours, they've been having meetings," you offer.

"We like all the TV sets. Danny thinks they are significant," Zero noted.

"Does he think Jesus is going come back as a game show host?" you asked.

"We're just looking for a sign, that's all," said Zero.

Danny did not enjoy the summer evenings he and Frannie would spend walking the beach. He didn't like sand and he didn't like the scuffs which the rocks and cans would inflict on his dress shoes.

You think Danny is being romantic, which is why you feel like a third wheel. But Danny is really just being kind, hoping that the nice cool Lake Erie breeze will clear out her sinuses which always made her so nervous and prone to headaches.

The sailboats are moored in front of the ghost town entertainment complex. Their noses are all obediently facing the exact same heading.

Frannie is talking to Danny while she rubs her temples.

"It's not a headache, it's a fullness Danny. It's like being in a little room with you on one of your tirades." She makes him feel cute.

Danny is practically blushing. He's so proud of how irritating he can be, as if this is an attractive quality. "Maybe we should try a different doctor," Danny suggests.

"I'm sick of doctors. If you go to a doctor it's his job to find something and I don't want anyone to find anything in me," Frannie explains.

"Maybe he'll find an enormous brain," Danny jokes.

"I don't want an enormous brain! I want one just like yours," she teases. "A little one."

"And you know what they say about the size of a man's brain?" you try to be funny.

"Or is it the size of his foot, I never get it right," you admit and continue quietly on your way, dropping back a few paces so you don't get in the middle of anything further.

Danny laughs but decides that he is going to call her brother and between the two of them, they are going to take her to a doctor, if for no other reason than so she won't annoy him with these walks any more.

"This ain't Bermuda," Danny reminds her.

"You're not Robert Redford," she reminds him.

"What?" he asks.

"This is good enough, that's all I mean," she answers and Danny is silenced by the pleasure of recognizing that all his smoke and mirrors may be a lot of hokum, but she is very true. Nothing else needs to be real.

You look back to them and you see hope and pain. You wonder how much of each is just a reflection of your own wishes and frustrations. How much of yourself do you wish you could see in each of them?

Father Terry Mulroy is riding a tired Schwinn 3-speed through the old Parish and comes upon the aged and neglected park on the river, three short blocks north of St. Matt's. Toledo is too small a town to have a significant inner-city, so this five-block area serves as the inner-city for all. A handful of nationals from a handful of countries live, work and play side-by-side, having no apparent ethnic status aside from simply being immigrants, country of origin of no concern to the average passer-by.

He sees an Asian woman sitting alone on a child's swing which barely moves with the light breeze. Her silky black hair is so pure that individual strands rise and surf the summer air without disturbing their brothers and sisters.

Mulroy quietly gets off the red and blue bicycle, and the flaking chrome suspension spring balancing the frame on the fat front tire interrupts the solace with a sigh of relief.

The woman's eyes are closed. She is a dove, gently defying gravity and abandoning her poverty as she rolls back and forth to nature's slow, deliberate rhythm.

Mulroy can hardly detect the wind which keeps her in motion, and the beautiful 30 year old woman wearing only something very short and black with the exception of a crimson red leather belt seems completely absorbed by it.

The Father squats on his knees behind and to the left of the woman, like he's kneeling before a Buddha. And he too is absorbed by the moment as a favorite image builds inside him.

He is standing beside an enormous skyscraper, one with no design to it whatsoever. It stands tall and completely rectangular. There are no indentations for the windows. There is no entrance. He stands frozen at its base as it silently falls to its side, slowly filling his vision with its magnitude, quietly falling – descending upon him.

"I am responsible for my own actions!" "I am not a cog. I am not part of a collective being!" "I can not abdicate my soul to God!"

The voice behind the voice which labors with his daily thoughts speaks to strengths and resentments of years gone by.

He sees beautiful colors as he rubs his closed eyes with the rolled knuckles of each hand.

"Ye shall see heaven open, and the angels of God ascending and descending upon the Son of man," the soft, velvety voice breaks the silence without disrupting his trance. She blends in to the moment and becomes one with the glory of a man's refusal to deny the significance of his own existence. "Oh, the burden of individuality," he laments.

He feels the beautiful woman's hands on his temples. Her face bows down from behind him and a single kiss is graced upon his forehead.

"I'm glad you have returned after so long," she whispers as her fingers caress his thin red hair.

"I don't know for certain what draws me to you," he answers as softly.

She nods her head in understanding. "Are you still..." he asks.

"I am still a whore, yes," she replies.

"Have you seen Danny?" he asks.

"No, I wanted to but I felt he is better off without me," she pivots around to look in his tired eyes.

"How is he?" she is genuinely curious in a personal way.

"He is looking for Jesus," he says as if they didn't both know how unlikely a task that would be for the enigmatic man.

"Jesus?" Mary exclaims.

"He goes to St. Matt's almost every day and stands vigil with the people there," Mulroy explains.

"This is not the Danny I know," he adds.

"I think this is the Danny that I know," she smiles.

He stands up, puts his hands on her shoulders. Although Mulroy soars above her like a tall oak, he is small in her company. Like a willow, his prominence at this moment is how near the earth his branches fall, how real his tears.

"This is unimaginable to me," he is quickly serious.

"Danny seeking the Lord?" she is plainly entertained.

"To what ends I wonder," he is less entertained.

"You said that if the Lord wasn't real we would invent him," she reminds him, privately noting how quickly these memories of his lessons return.

"Left to his own devices, I am somewhat nervous about the type of Lord Danny might invent for us," he smiles.

"He'd probably be a good Lord. A tall Lord!" she laughs.

"He'd certainly be a very forgiving one if he's Danny's invention," Mulroy adds.

"And a miracle a minute!" she delights to conjure up the notion.

"A miracle a minute," he repeats. "Would you like to see him? Maybe you could help," he suggests.

"Danny may be looking for Jesus, but I doubt that Jesus is looking for me. I think Danny and I are better apart," she answers sadly.

"If Danny needed me, I would be there for him," she adds, her eyes echoing a certain longing for the past and laughing with a certain time-worn glint that shows how much fun the old times had been.

"You were always the special one for him. I don't know why. It seems you hardly knew each other.

"Maybe that is why," she suggests.

"Can I ask, did you love him?"

"He made me laugh. I've known women to think they were in love with less of a feeling," her smile reveals a weak left side that is pleasantly imperfect.

"You sought out privacy so you could laugh?!" he asks.

"Joking is his mating call. You've never known him like I have," she teases.

"I'll be careful with my laughter from here on," he shares the thought.

"Do you think he loves me?" she asks and becomes instantly vulnerable.

"I think he sincerely does," Father Mulroy assures her.

"And the other woman?"

"Frannie," Father Mulroy reminds her.

"Yes?"

"He sincerely loves her too," the priest answers honestly.

"How can he love two women?" she asks.

"Danny is a very sincere man," he shrugs.

She would never have detected his sincerity or his manliness from his lovemaking. Danny would meet her and suffer the agony of paying to do so. She would bring him close and pantomime the theater of foreplay, but before he could accept it for truth, before he could fool himself in to believing this was love, he recognized the absurdity of sex with a stranger and reconciled himself to becoming familiar in a different way.

He felt odd because he could not be cold and callous at the time when he felt a real man should be.

It always seemed exciting in concept, but in practice, it was just another berserk aspect of life. Mary Chu would quickly succumb and he didn't seem to mind if neither of them found the experience satisfying. "How satisfying could you expect this to be?" he would ask.

Nevertheless, as Danny's relationship with Frannie was evolving in to a delightful love affair that was somehow too pleasant for any penetrating intimacies, Mary Chu's friendship let him feel more challenged, more at odds with his own nature.

"Do you consider this cheating?" she would ask, regarding his devotion to Frannie versus his time spent with her.

"What am I cheating her out of?" he would respond.

"Good point," she would laugh as she grabbed a handful of his lifelessness.

Danny liked to fulfill expectations with quick, broad strokes so he could get on with the parts of his plan which would make him memorable and exceptional among the small thinkers of the planet.

"You'll know the right time when it comes, Mary Chu. Every person is here for a special moment." Mulroy brushes his fingers on her cheek and Mary

Chu turns and walks away with a smile on her face. She looks back to see that Father Mulroy is on his bicycle and is pedaling away, and she enjoys a quiet sigh, and smiles at a gentleness greater than any pain she had ever known.

Father Mulroy knows she is more than a prostitute and she knows he is less than a saint. They both know that Danny DeMarco is just another regular guy trying to push the big boulder up the steep hill of futility.

She remembers that life creates its own self-sustaining breath, and reminds herself that a train does not require tracks behind it to go forward.

She at that moment makes a private pledge. A painted rainbow colors itself in her mind. She closes her eyes and feels her lips smile. A voice says "I love you," and another responds with that warmth we only know as promise.

Danny has met with the church group many times and he has promised them that a very big moment is about to arrive. They would be content with a nice lunch.

Bishop Flagg has been shocked by a phone call he received from a violently angered Father Pat. "He came to you through me in good faith. And I did not know that we employed a goon squad!" his words were thin and squealy, his emotions stretched taut from a lifetime of restraint.

"He had no right to the idea and certainly not to the subsequent manufacturing process," responded Bishop Flagg while squinting at the latest numbers, tapping his polished fingernail on the line that says MISC. INCOME.

Bishop Hutt was in his glory, and Flagg was at the height of his game. With the new souvenir scheme in full operation, his projections proved conservative. The last call he had from the Vatican was quite rewarding. "The world is good," said the small peaceful voice. "Is the puppy really cured?" he asked.

"We're right on target," reported Hutt.

Danny is not at Talk of the Town tonight. He has become a videographer, for some reason, wandering the streets of Toledo with a video camera strapped to his shoulder.

Finding his target, he fires away, the little bulb blasting an irritating light toward his object, a hamburger stand. He looks like a bathysphere.

"Hey Mister, are you making a movie?" a young Black girl wanders in front of the camera and makes her big screen debut.

"You're in the picture," he scolds her.

"I'm in your movie?" she gasps with excitement.

"Yeah, you're the star," he zooms past her toward a tighter shot of the hamburger place.

She walks away thinking that there is always good reason to believe in tomorrow.

"Talk of the Town," you answer the phone because Danny's in the can.

"My ants still aren't here," the tired voice recites to you over the phone. He never asks who you are.

"Hold on," you say, and after muffling the receiver with your palm, you tell Danny "It's someone about ants," and you hope that this will have nothing to do with you.

"Father Matt from St. Pat's, or is it Father Pat from St. Matt's," Danny says to Father Mulroy.

"Father Pat," Mulroy assures him.

"Oh. Father Pat!!!" and Danny rushes to the phone.

"I'll get you some ants. Are you ready to work with me?" Danny is practically swallowing the receiver.

Father Pat has spent many more hours than usual staring off in to space. What used to be a time of deliberation has become a time of avoidance, substituting emptiness for realization of the truth.

The truth being that this little square of pathos over which he reigns is no symbol of trust or endearment between him and the Bishop, much less anyone above him. The phone never rings and it never shall.

Thankfully the silence and the emptiness has great enormity, albeit no content, and the truth is easily and unnoticeably swallowed up within it.

"No ants," the voice responds in tired fashion.

"By tonight you'll have ants. That's a guarantee. Danny at Talk of the Town takes care of his boys. You can see that, huh?" Danny works the situation like a corner man at a bar fight.

"Get me my ants and I'll help you," the old Father accepts the deal, having no idea what his part might amount to.

"Delusion is almost as tangible as reality. An answer is almost as tangible as a question. Everything in our minds is chemical, so as long as the chemistry is stirring, the protagonist is real," rationalizes the tired man. And he smiles because there is truth to his tapestry and a feeling caused by one stimulation is as valid as a feeling caused by any other.

Feelings are fully validated once felt.

An hour later Danny bursts into Harry's apartment where Harry is lamenting the decidedly bad attitude he's noticed in Queen Isadora.

"Harry, I need some ants right now. Can you spare a colony or so?" Danny pleads.

"Isadora here is not happy, Danny, I'm concerned," Harry says.

"Give me Isadora and a bag of others and I'll get them started in a 12-step group," Danny promises.

"What do you need them for?" asks Harry.

"It's a religious matter," says Danny. And Harry, finding this perfectly reasonable says "I can put together a family with Isadora here if it's important to you. Where will they live?"

"St. Matt's. They can be the first ants to join the Church. Can you take them there and talk to the priest there about the ants?" asks Danny.

"I'll give you some ants but I am not taking them to church, Danny. How's my sister?" Harry looks him in the eye, but not in an accusing manner.

"Okay. And she's fine, still gets those headaches from time to time but I think it's all in her head," answers Danny.

At 8 pm, Danny and the plastic sandwich bag of ants strolls in to St. Matt"s. Danny could swear he hears them yelping. He's finishing up a bologna sandwich, bites off a little morsel and drops it in the bag as an act of kindness, but doesn't realize that he has decapitated an unsuspecting victim who dies on contact with the cold cut.

Queen Isadora is already out-of-sorts for being transported in such a common manner, and goes completely berserk when she sees one of her recent lovers killed before nature had taken its course and put him under in its own way.

A scrappy voice immerses out of the dark chapel.

"What do you have there, Danny?" Half-Pint asks in that cute half-stupor drawl of his.

"Ants," answers Danny.

Half-Pint accepts this and slips into unconsciousness.

Danny knocks at Father Pat's door and enters.

"Father Pat. Your ants have arrived!" he exclaims, and for the next hour, Father Pat gently places each ant, one by one, in the priest's Uncle Milton's Ant Farm, welcoming each of them individually to his Parish.

Queen Isadora is finally lifted in the air by his scraggly fingers and begins screaming her lungs out at his gentle smiling face.

"I don't want to be a nun!!!" she yelps. "I use birth control!" "I like sex with animals!!!" "I covet my mother!!!" He drops her gently on the white sand and she embarrasses herself by toppling over while the rest of her new clan are hitting the dirt like professional parachutists.

"You are a man of God," says Father Pat as he embraces Danny.

"You wanted ants, I got you ants, a whole civilization!" boasts Danny.

On the way out, Danny is satisfied that he's made a hit with Father Pat.

"What can I do in return?" he asks.

Danny explains in depth. Queen Isadora overhears the entire thing and slaps her forehead in amazement. A new lover saunters over to her ready to break in the new digs.

"Take a hike!" says the Queen as she deliberates

about Danny's unbelievable request.

Danny is on his way out when he hears an excited old voice coming from behind. The old priest has chased him toward the sanctuary. "You're a real savior," he thanks Danny again most fondly.

"A real savior?" Danny hears Zero repeating the Priest's words.

"Real enough for now," Danny tells him.

"When is the first meeting?" asks the Priest.

"Soon. I can feel it, they all can. The time is near," says Danny as he slowly and confidently strolls out.

Queen Isadora's royal needs are fooling with her brain and she's got all her hopeful beaus in a Conga line surrounding her, just to let her enjoy their various physical advantages.

She's doing her best to rise above recent occurrences, so she allows her mind to dwell instead on her disappointment in how men really don't last as long as they used to.

Chapter Twenty Seven

Danny walks into Talk of the Town carrying his presentation briefcase and matching aluminum stand. His shoes were spit-shined over at Short Hairs.

JoAnn Conroy's son, Darryl, is hiding from the Army recruiters who promised him a chance to learn a craft involving high explosives. But he didn't show up for enlistment last Wednesday because he doesn't like men squeezing his testicles.

He's insulted that the Army insists on putting him through such embarrassing procedures, especially considering how much experience he brings to the picture.

Ever since Darryl was a kid, there was a certain incendiary weirdness about him. While other kids were studying writing and adding, Darryl applied himself to setting harmless but bewildering fires in odd places. Chief among those were his neighbors' hedges and various bulletin boards in the school hallways.

Last summer, a low budget Hollywood movie came to town and they put him on in the special effects department assisting the crazed Yakov Blum, who set the Maumee River on fire, and blew up the neighboring Watershed Restaurant just for good measure.

"The restaurant wasn't in the script, but I couldn't resist," Darryl would later explain with a sparkle in his eye. "I hated those big carrot chunks they served with everything on the menu," he complained.

But to right things with the world, Darryl is presently putting in some serious servitude, biding his time operating the shoe shine concession at the salon. Few non-females brave the bleachy, sulfury odor to get their shoes attended to, so Darryl has become a good, long listener.

"I'm going to need your help," says Danny as Darryl scratches his nose with a brown waxed index finger, and then smudges it about with his knuckle.

"I'm good at blowing things up, Danny," he answers errantly.

"That's very nice, Darryl," Danny assures him.

"Are you making a movie?" he asks.

"Let's just say there's going to be a celebration."

Danny has had enough of this conversation, satisfied that Darryl and a host of others will be very available when the time comes.

"Your sister does wonders with rollers," says Danny as he watches the large goldfish shaped body maneuver itself out of the chair and smile wretchedly toward him, her freshly painted lips popping open from being stuck together by the cheap coloring agent.

"My sister was robbed by those movie people, Danny. That movie belonged to her and what did they bring in, some practically bald-headed slut from

Los Angeles," Darryl growls. "If she knew anything about hair, she'd have some!"

Danny stands up and admires the mirror shine, his reflection seeming high above the black leather, giving him the illusion of height.

Danny tips Darryl 50 cents for which Darryl is repulsed even though he's used to big talk and small rewards.

"Thanks much," he mutters.

"There's more where that came from," promises Danny.

On his short walk back to Talk of the Town, Danny is absorbed with his own reflection in the newly shined shoes. He notices that he looks rather sullen but figures that this is because his head is drooping, so he lifts it suddenly to face the troops.

Father Mulroy, Zeke, Frannie and you. The core.
The family. The place could be sealed up, air tight,
and it would form its own self-sustaining eco-system,
the embodiment of every form of trade, friendship
and servitude.

You've come a long way, however, and this is a
promised moment. Danny said that today you would
graduate from customer to partner. Frannie was told
she would be elevated from special buddy to management. Father Mulroy wants nothing but isn't in a
hurry to leave.

Danny closes the door and locks it tight. He drops
the blinds that have "Closed For Inventory" sten-
ciled on the outside. Those blinds were left over
from when the previous tenant's soda fountain was
closed up by the IRS for back taxes. But the owner,
disappeared and was never seen or heard from again.
"Wealthiest motherfucker in Argentina" he remem-
bered the words of investment advisor, Dolores
Irons.

Danny always felt a certain affinity toward Herb,
even though he had never met him. Oh, sure, there
was the common suspicion that Herb had become
the only Jewish Nazi sympathizer. No wonder the
man had a reputation for being confused and possibly suicidal.

Had Herb paid his taxes, Danny would still be
promoting fallen music acts in small and fallen cities

where the public has to be thankful for what it gets.

"This here's a day of infamy," declares Danny to his flock. You are wearing those goofy painter's pants, the off-white ones with enough pockets and loops to fit a table setting for twelve. The only thing in them is your thin blue fabric wallet with the cool Velcro closure, and a small soft-bound book entitled *Dips I Have Known,* your last recipe book ever, you hope.

"Al, first of all I want to welcome you to the staff," Danny announces.

You've already quit your job at the cook book place, just in the nick of time because they were about to get rid of you.

"I've had enough of your complaining!" your boss had said last week. Actually, the Milton Mallet book has been going badly, the talk show host demanding that you start it off with his mother's favorite recipe for breakfast. "Rice and milk, a little butter on top, warm it up, eat it," was how Mallet described the preparation procedure to you.

"This book is going to be a big joke!" you explained.

"It doesn't matter! Even if it's filled with recipes for chocolate milk, it'll sell. Just put it into words and stop annoying me!" the boss turned and walked away.

"You know, some people just don't know the

value of having a paycheck," he muttered from the distance.

You're feeling very glad to be part of Danny's team.

Father Mulroy hasn't shaved for a few days and his face's little ragged rivers and streams have tiny, thin red reeds growing in them.

Frannie is wearing her customary loose-fitting jeans and a floppy white blouse which lets you catch an occasional glimpse of her baby blue bra, a treat which does not arouse you but which pleases your senses, and you do not feel a bit cheated that her private parts are forbidden to your touch.

You could swear that you can see a trace of her nipples, and this is a big sexual moment for you.

Danny, blessed with a charisma that is so big it gets there before him, stands up on a bar stool, clears his throat and speaks to the attentive audience.

"We're going to be having some meetings here, and I am going to ask that all of you participate," he declares.

"Is this the Jesus thing you've been doing?" Zeke asks.

"Jesus thing?" Danny mimics. "Jesus thing. We're talking about a moment that has been prayed for since the beginning of time. This is not just a thing. I have a sense. So do many others. It's not a thing!"

he lectures.

"We're accustomed to having the more well-to-do level of market served at this establishment. What I mean by that is people who have jobs and the where-with-all to buy a few drinks. The members of these meetings have shed themselves of such earthly goods and are basically going to be drinking on the house," he explains.

None of you look at each other. None of you would know what attitude would be okay to express.

"There's three dozen of them, 36. In fact, they call themselves The 36, and what they are doing here is organizing the search," he continues.

"And they are searching for the Messiah?" you ask incredulously.

"They are looking for the truth. It's what everyone is looking for, except these people are special. Gifted."

"Jesus H. Christ!" says Frannie. "All of a sudden, you have decided it's time to find Jesus!"

"What's the H stand for?" you ask.

"I don't know! Herb. Horace. I don't know! Ask him when you find him!" she quips.

"Well, laugh all you'd like, Frannie! Do you have a better idea on how to invest our time? Maybe you'd prefer we search for cute earrings and new panty hose colors," Danny attacks.

Frannie gets very nervous and starts breathing in

little, clearly unfulfilling efforts.

"I know you aren't like that, Frannie, I'm just saying that's how some people waste away their lives, and we're done with that," he apologizes.

"Are these people serious?" Zeke asks.

"They are searching for their savior, for the Lord, Jesus Christ, and I'm helping," Danny explains.

"This is very nice of you, Danny. I'm sorry for before," says Frannie with a half smile and a quick sideways glance over to you. You share the private moment and hope she'll bend down for a second.

"They'll be here any minute, so let's team up and make this work," asks Danny. "They need our faith," he says. "They need to know we believe in them," he solemnly concludes.

There is a meek knock on the door and almost immediately another. You turn to look at the door and a round, grimy, toothless smile entertains you with a wry grin.

"We're closed! Go away!!" Zeke rises to the occasion, and the childish adult's face gasps with surprise.

"No! That's them!! One minute, Zero, just one minute!" Danny rushes to the door, his shiny feet glistening, adhering to the air. You expect him to dance on point in any second.

The door opens and a parade of street people strolls in like a band of Gypsies. The only common denominator seems to be a certain musty odor and a singular sensation of having traveled very far without having moved a centimeter.

"My friends, these are – The 36," Danny presents his crew.

"Lamed Vav" mutters Father Mulroy.

"What's Lamed Vav?" asks Frannie as the crew is ushered in. "That's us!" says Pinky as she eyes the horse's head. "Unbeknownst to us, we are attuned to the return of Jesus, and..."

"And they have all become attuned at the same time, so the time seems very near," Danny finishes for Pinky.

Pinky can't take her eye off the horse. "Is this a bear or something?" she asks.

"Fundamentally, it's a horse," says Half-Pint. "Fundamentally, it's a dead horse," adds Zero. "Who's Pope?" asks Half-Pint.

"He's the guy in the white dress. I seen him on TV, no matter what's going on, he waves," comments Pinky.

"No matter what is going on, wars, holocausts, depressions, the Pope is doing his thing, waving hello," says Danny. "We can't be bothered with him any more.

"Excuse me Danny, but you're being kind of nasty," Frannie is the only one who could say this, and she had to.

He whips his head around and aims those dark pupils at her.

"Nasty? You're calling me nasty because I don't have reverence for the Pope? For Pope on the Rope? For Pope on the T-Shirt. For Pope on the Parade???"

"I'm not nasty toward the Pope. He's had to stand in until the real deal came along. What we're all saying here today, tell me if I'm wrong, is that the real deal is on our doorstep!" Danny rallies the troops.

"So why's the Pope's baseball hat on the horse?" asks Pinky, whose tongue bursts through a wad of gum stretched like a storm door around her teeth.

"It was just an idea," Danny steps in and leads them to their seats.

You are watching and listening while magnificently colorful images of steamed cauliflower and caramelized onions being placed gently on fresh pizza dough struggle for attention inside your brain. Recipe editing seems a more rational career choice at the moment. Maybe ghostwriting is the ultimate nobility. Perhaps you were hasty.

"We all sense that the time is here. It could even happen tonight. We're decent and dedicated," Danny speaks to the 36.

"Decency we got. Food we don't got," complains Zero.

"Food you got starting now. But I want you to concentrate on our main purpose," Danny lectures.

"And what a purpose!" remarks Mulroy.

"To know when Jesus comes back," Danny explains.

"Jesus is here, in the heart," says Frannie and you are jealous of her palm as it presses against her bosom.

"Tell them where Jesus really is." Danny asks Mulroy, who figures that this is a nice time to share a bit of knowledge. Esteem from such a motley crew seems oddly precious.

Father Mulroy gets off his stool and stands before the congregation.

"It was said that those who would first recognize him would be men and women of the most humble vocation. They would not know that they are spiritual people," he explains.

"I've never been on a vocation," Half-Pint notes.

"That's vacation!" Zero remarks.

"Never been on one of those either," Half-Pint responds proudly. His bushy eyebrows flicker up and down his forehead.

"Well, we are humble. We have nothing," adds Pinky.

"Maybe that's the idea. You have nothing to distract you from the Divine Presence," Mulroy remarks.

"Divine Presence!" Danny is absolutely gleeful. "Divine Presence, that's what you share, now let's concentrate and ask ourselves deep down inside 'Where is Jesus Christ?'" Danny leads the group.

They all close their eyes tightly, except for Half-Pint who closes only the eye closest to Danny, using the other one to eye Dayglow, the dwarfish purple-haired woman wrapped in several layers of stadium blankets, a yellow squirt container of mustard hanging out of her left pocket, a couple of feet of brown and green macramé wrapped around her waist.

"I know that he's near," she whispers to Half-Pint who finds her very attractive in body and mind.

Half-Pint's eyebrows tap out a note of interest.

"I think maybe I've seen him," it occurs to Half-Pint.

"Where'd you see him?" asks Zero.

"At church."

"That's not Jesus. That's the Jesus on the cross. Jesus the statue." Zero explains.

"He didn't look like the Jesus on the cross," Half-Pint notes thoughtfully.

"This is 2,000 years later. It's the new Jesus!" Zero comments.

Everyone is contorting themselves. It's been a long time since any of them had to concentrate on anything and most of them weren't sure how to do it, but they knew what it looked like when people thought hard. One guy was actually squeezing the folds of skin on his forehead together like someone trying to wink the wrong eye.

"What's the deal, Danny?" you ask.

"These people have been waiting all their lives for him," Danny answers.

"So, you're going to start a manhunt?" you risk his scorn but you can't contain your concern. "I think the Pope idea was more implementable," you try to add some positive alternative direction.

"Too much legal hassle," Danny leers at you. Zeke adds his thoughts.

"Just because the Pope idea didn't fly, I think it's premature to go in there with Jesus at this point in time," he has considered this at length.

"Danny, can I ask you something in private?" you whisper.

"Sure," he says and you walk to the back room where the embroidery computer used to be.

"Danny, these people are taking you seriously, you know," you reveal to him.

"They should!" he answers softly. "The Father says there's Jesus in all of us, so maybe we find the nearest one who has the highest Jesus content," he elaborates.

"Well, that's a thought," you admit.

"Good, so stick with me from that point of view and don't bother with any integrity issues. We're going beyond that sort of thing. This isn't the cook book business!" he reminds you.

"Integrity was not an issue there," you remind him.

"Point made!" he gloats.

"I see," you say, but you don't really.

"Unbelievable things can come of this," he concludes as you rejoin the group.

This, you believe.

"Let's find out how the group feels about our efforts," Danny shrugs his shoulders innocently and addresses the crew.

"Group, do you believe in our Lord Jesus Christ?" and they all raise their hands and go ooh and ahhh. "Can we eat now?" asks Zero, and they all raise their hands even higher.

"Are you the people, the real people?" Danny asks for another response, to which they respond very positively.

"Humble vocationers," Half-Pint announces proudly.

"And is Jesus here looking out for you?" he asks one last question.

"If we are going to be actually eating a sit-down meal, that's a miracle, so Jesus must be somewhere near," answers Pinkie.

"How many of you agree?' Danny asks.

They all raise their hands. "I can feel him in my bones," declares Half-Pint. "Jesus is here, we just have to find him," says Dayglow.

"I'd like to meet him when you find him," Frannie asks politely. "Do you think I could, Danny?" she nudges him.

"This is possibly blasphemous," you mention to Danny in a whisper.

"How can this be blasphemous????!!!!" he screams.

"The entire world of Christianity is 100% based on Jesus coming back and these good people say he's already here!!! What are we supposed to do? Let him hang out waiting for the world to catch on? How's he going to find an apartment, get a job? You want Jesus sitting around reading the classifieds?" Danny is beet red.

"Let's suppose He is here," Danny reasons. "Supposing that He is, can you imagine how He must feel being totally ignored? A little more of this kind of treatment and He might just take off again on us," he explains.

"Then there'd have to be a third coming," Father Mulroy says dryly.

"Eeek, we gotta find Him," Zero declares.

"Where do you look?" asks Frannie?

"We go to the streets again tonight and if we don't find Him, we meet again here tomorrow night," Danny instructs and everyone seems to find this reasonable.

"Can we eat now?" asks Zero and everyone smiles.

"Maybe this will be the last supper," suggests

Pinky.

"Last!? It's my first since I was 11," laughs Half-Pint. "Sit- down, that is," he elaborates.

They chow down their chicken and mashed potatoes, and no one complains that the silverware is plastic. "How about some liquid refreshment?" suggests Half-Pint, to which Danny remarks, "No chance. We're on a holy mission."

**Chapter
Twenty
Nine**

Frannie is in bed. Danny is in the bathroom reading army jokes in Readers Digest. He finished using the toilet half an hour ago, but it's his favorite reading chair and he doesn't mind the breeze.

"Frannie, listen to this. Can you hear me out there?" he bellows.

"I don't feel so good, Danny," she calls back.

"Okay, but listen anyway," he says, accustomed to the fact that Frannie never feels all that good ever. Feeling not so good is about as good as she ever feels.

"Okay, Danny. I'm listening," she answers, her head buried in a pillow, squooshed around her ears to relieve the pressure.

"An army Private is stringing telephone wire out in the middle of nowhere along with his Sergeant. The Sergeant is up in the pole and the Private gets bit in his private parts by a rattlesnake."

"Frannie, are you listening? This is a good one," he calls to her.

"Yes, I'm listening," she answers although her mind is more on the search for Jesus and how seriously they all are pursuing it.

"The Sergeant calls up the medic with his portable handset and asks what to do. The medic says you just make a little cut then you suck out the venom. So, you know what the Sergeant says to the Private?" Danny asks.

"What's he say, Danny?" she volunteers.

"He says, 'They said you're going to die'!" get it Frannie, do you get it?" Danny is practically bouncing in glee on the toilet seat.

Frannie is thinking that the world could use a little Jesus right now.

"That's a good one, Danny," she offers as she falls asleep between her pillows, her last thought being that Danny is not as guilty of anything as one would think.

**Chapter
Thirty**

They were in to their sixth night, and still not a glimpse at the Messiah.

Danny had to keep up their faith. Everyone was a bit on edge, and the hot dogs and potato chip dinner was not heightening any spirits. The pretzels made no big impression either.

"Listen, do you believe in Jesus Christ?" Danny asks the group as they finish gobbling down their dinner.

"Of course we believe, but can we talk about these meals?" risks Zero.

"Of course," Danny answers quickly.

"The church is better," Zero confides. We get potatoes and a vegetable there.

"Yeah, well, is the church helping you find Jesus?" Danny challenges.

"That is the idea, Danny," Father Mulroy offers.

"I think tonight could be the night," Danny announces. "Now, do we all believe in the second coming?" he asks again.

Frannie looks up and whispers to Danny so God doesn't hear her even responding to such a question: "We all believe in Jesus," she assures him. "Don't you?" she asks.

"I think I've made my case very clear on that point," Father Mulroy reminds all of you.

"I've never believed in him more," Danny answers with a manic smile.

The last time you've seen this zany expression on Danny's face was when he returned from his presentation of the Pope souvenir idea.

"We've got to look for a sign," says Danny as he turns off the lights and turns on the televisions. As they warm up, you see the black and white static starting to take the shape of a horse.

"I'm getting a vision," says Pinkie.

"Me too!" says Half-Pint as he opens one eye and glances at the monitors.

"It's Trigger!" declares Pinkie.

"It's the same horse that's wearing the Pope hat!" says Zero.

"I don't think Jesus rode a horse." You hate to break the mood so you share your concerns privately with Zeke who is busy chewing the brown outside coating off the pretzels.

"This doesn't mean he's on a horse! It's a symbol, can't you see?" Danny answers.

"It looks like the Marlboro man to me," notes Pinky. "I like a man who always wears boots" she adds.

"I prefer a man who's gotten rid of them ," Frannie shrugs.

"What's that have to do with anything?" Danny brushes her off.

"Well, I see a horse, that's all I know," you comment.

"Does everyone have a vision of a horse? Are we sharing something important here?" Danny works the crowd.

They all nod in agreement. They are surrounded by a picture of a concrete horse, with the real horse's head leering down on them, even being dead, it's suspicious of this whole thing.

"Follow me, I know what you're describing," Danny cheers everyone to their feet and they follow him out the door. They walk past the Toledo Barber College where Emma Cheeks is giving her first facial to old Farley Humple, who is imagining that she's kneading him elsewhere. Her attention is diverted by the parade following Danny down the street, and her hands clasp around his face causing Farley to feel her soft belly touching the back of his head, and he is rendered delirious.

"Where ya going?" she asks through the screen window.

"What are you, a cop?" Danny sneers at her as he leads the band down the street, around the corner, a left, a right, down another street and then he points toward the building where the street dead-ends.

"Crazy people," she smiles.

"Nothing but trouble," says Farley. "Communists!" he declares. "Get those hands back here," he demands.

You are momentarily jealous of the old guy

squirming at her innocent touch. You could use a simple little pleasure right now as you follow the crowd. You can see the outline of a gigantic cigarette billboard with a rugged cowboy on a fearless stallion taunting young boys to become real men by sucking in smoke without coughing.

Father Pat is carrying out his end of the bargain. After sharing a few thoughts with the Queen, he walks out to the street and follows the map which Danny provided him.

At the same time, Danny's parade rolls its way toward the violet illumination up ahead.

The tired spotlights planted in the crumbling asphalt point high in the air over the shanty of a burger joint with the enormous Marlboro billboard balancing precariously on its roof.

"He's there!" Zero jumps up and down. "It's the vision!"

"Bethlehem!!!" Half-Pint sees it too.

"Are you sure this is it?" Danny asks as he looks at you and furls his brow just as you are about to ask what the nature of this prank actually is.

They all march up to Rodeo Burger and enter the place following Danny's lead. "Do you see him?" Danny asks the frenetic soldiers, as his eyes scan the room robotically.

"Over there!!!!" Danny points toward the corner by the mens' room.

At that moment, Father Pat is staring at the bombastic structure, completely baffled by why the map led him to this place. He enters and sees Danny and his congregation, and he joins them from behind. No one notices him.

Danny is pointing at Fran's brother Harry.

Zero gets on his knees and everyone follows. Harry looks up from his classified ads. "Check!" he looks to the waitress who's pupils are both aimed in opposite directions.

"Jesus Christ, Superstar, " mutters Zero.

"It is very unlikely that this is Jesus," Father Mulroy whispers to Danny.

"Not according to those who know," says Danny as he points to the flock of parishioners breathtaken by the view of Harry gobbling down the last of his Rodeo burger.

"Harry is the Lord our God?" Frannie is taken aback, wondering just who she is as a result.

"Well, now you know what the H stands for," answers Danny.

"Harry? Jesus Harry Christ? Wow! Does that make me someone?" she asks Danny.

"Yes, it makes you the daughter of God," Danny answers solemnly.

Meanwhile Harry is backing up against the men's room door. He's pretty sure these are bill collectors who have finally decided to attack as one unified force, like N.A.T.O.

Danny pushes his way through the throng and puts his arm around Harry's shoulder. "What is going on here, Harry?" Danny asks.

"I don't know," Harry is petrified.

"What do you want from this man?" Danny asks the crowd.

"I'd like all the bubble gum in the whole world," says Pinkie.

"I'd like peace on earth and a Rodeo Burger medium rare," asks Half-Pint.

"I would only ask him for a chance to make more of myself," says Zero.

"Harry, why are they asking you for these things?" Danny questions the baffled Harry.

"He's Jesus Christ!" declares Pinkie.

"Jesus. Jesus! Jesus!!" they all chant.

"They say you're Jesus," Danny tells Harry.

"I'm not Jesus," Harry tells them all.

"I'm Harry. I raise ants," he goes on the offensive.

"Ants!!!" an old, excited voice breaks in. It's Father Pat. "Is he – is he –" he can't get the words out, but Danny helps him.

"Yes, Father, this is Harry. It is a remarkable twist of fate that Harry appears to have been tracked down by this holy gathering and proclaimed our Messiah. Father, can you explain this, can it be true?" he beseeches Father Pat.

Father Pat walks up to Harry and studies him carefully.

"You should have told us they were carpenter ants. They ate their way out of their Uncle Milton's Ant Farm."

"Is the Queen okay?" asks Harry as the onlookers are getting fidgety wondering when Jesus starts performing some miracles. Half-pint is by the window staring at the sky hoping for at least an unscheduled eclipse.

"She's fine. See for yourself," and he pulls a little medicine container out of his pocket where Isadora is just sitting there, seething with anger. She takes one look at Harry and could just spit.

"I'll get you more," Harry promises.

"Carpenter ants!" exclaims Zero. "Carpenter, get it? Carpenter. Son of God."

"Jesus loves his little children, all the children in the world!" they all start singing.

The crowd continues their chanting and singing and they raise Harry up in the air as they carry him out the door. Danny, Father Mulroy, Frannie and you follow. Father Pat is behind you, holding his ant vial out in front of him like it's a beacon of some sort.

"I am not Jesus!!! I don't do any miracles! I can't even get a job!!!" he pleads, but the evidence is apparently overwhelming.

"Harry! Harry!!" Frannie calls to her brother. He is being turned around and around like a helicopter blade. "Harry!!!" she shouts to get his attention.

"Yes, Frannie?" he drops his head down and stares at her upside down.

"My head hurts bad, Harry."

"I can only cure blindness, sorry," he jokes.

Then he notices that she is breathing very rapidly and is gasping anxiously.

"Frannie, this is nothing to be concerned about. I'm sure we'll clear it up in the morning," he tells her as he is flung from side to side.

She sits on the curb and gathers herself. She smiles to Harry so he won't worry.

You find yourself more coherent than you would expect. "What we have here is a situation where we should pray that God is either very forgiving or has no access to serious weaponry," you tell the whoever can hear you.

"If it turns out that Harry isn't really Jesus, will God kill us?" Zeke asks Father Mulroy.

"He does that one way or another," Mulroy chuckles.

Harry has decided to enjoy this, waiting for them to let the cat out of the bag and let him know what's really going on. He is pretending he might be Superman, his arms out front and his body flying through the air over the heads of his many fans.

Danny just grins as he follows the pilgrimage back to Talk of the Town, Harry jittering in the sky like a painfully hooked tuna. Zero, Half-Pint and Pinkie leading the way, exclaiming to passerby's that they have found Jesus.

"Literally," Zero tells them, but the passerby's either ignore them or wish them well. One says "Tell him I watch all his television shows on Sunday."

Over the crowd, Danny can't help but be amused by the shrieking protestations coming from the fitful tuna.

"Danny! Help me!!! I'm not Jesus!!! Let me down, I'm not Jesus!!!" but he is hardly heard and not listened to by a single person except one passerby who comments to you that he's convinced.

They arrive at Talk of the Town where the still image of the rodeo horse remains on all the TV sets. Everyone gathers around Harry.

"All right, first and foremost I want to thank everyone for this exciting evening. I have my ants to tend to and let's call it a night," he tries to be calm.

Danny tells Father Pat that it all starts now. Father Pat is transfixed by a carpet beetle dashing between his legs. He sets Isadora down by his toe so she can pretend she's on an African Lion Safari.

The beetle knocks in to the medicine vial and Isadora is tossed against the side of the bottle by the tremor. She rights herself and walks away, with a vague aching in her left rear leg, which she attributes to that old family charley horse thing.

"Father Pat and Father Mulroy, both men of the cloth, I would ask you, number one, is there any record of Jesus Christ having claimed to be the Messiah?" Danny takes the floor.

"Jesus always denied it," Father Mulroy quickly responds. "He even denied being King of the Jews."

"And Harry?" Danny looks to Harry for his response.

"I am not the Messiah. I don't even know any Jews," Harry answers.

"Father Pat, when you add up the evidence, as a spokesman for the Church itself, what do we have here?" Danny then whistles to release Father Pat from Isadora's demonic gaze.

"If this is THE 36, then who could doubt it? The question is not whether he is Jesus but whether they are the 36," he confuses everyone.

"Well, there are 36 of us," adds Zero.

"And we all knew it at the same time," Half-pint joins in.

"What we need is a miracle," Danny breaks in. "We need a genuine miracle so there can be no question about the validity of this situation," he adds and then gestures for you to open the door, a moment you have not relished because there is a tinge of deceit to it.

Earlier Danny told you that we'd have to work Harry up to actual Jesus-hood, that Jesus was returning through Harry, not that Harry had always been Jesus. "That's why we need to sort of jump-start the miracle thing," Danny explained.

"This is Sarah Levy," you introduce the cute little girl wearing a white lace dress, white pantyhose and a white little flower in her hand.

"Sarah, what miracle have you prayed for?" Danny asks like he's hosting a TV marathon for some rare affliction.

"I would like to see," she purrs the sweet words from her innocent childish lips.

"Harry, come with me to the girl," Danny takes Harry's arm and Harry reluctantly follows. Everybody looks on quietly, hardly breathing for fear of interrupting his concentration.

"I can't do that!" Harry exclaims.

"Touch her forehead, close your eyes and concentrate, and say 'Heal!'," Danny directs him.

"That's ridiculous!" Harry retorts.

"Harry, do you think the prospect of eyesight is ridiculous to an eight year old girl who has never seen the sunset, has never enjoyed the colors of a flower garden, who has never witnessed a professional wrestling match?" Danny whispers.

Harry humors him, touches the girl's forehead and mutters "Heal," under his breath.

"With a little passion if you don't mind," Danny cajoles him.

"Okay, heal!!" he gives a bit more enthusiasm.

The little girl squeezes her closed eyes and rubs them with her hands. She slowly opens her eyes and is dumbfounded by the sight.

"I can see!" she exclaims. "I can see!!!"

"Tell him 'Thank you Jesus', Sarah," Danny has his arm softly around her shoulder, aiming her at Harry so she knows which one he is.

"Thank you Jesus," and Danny slides her over to you, and you quickly and smoothly cause her exit. You hand her over to her hysterically laughing teenage brother, palming him the $20 you promised him.

"You must be exhausted," Danny says to Harry, who is chugging a tall beer and flipping popcorn in to the air, trying to catch them with his mouth. "This is not very becoming for a Messiah," he whispers.

"Can I still call you Harry?" Danny asks as Harry slouches against the bar, the group now gone, convinced that their savior needs to rest up after almost 2000 years of waiting for them.

"I'm not Jesus," Harry mumbles like a punch-drunk fighter whose stubborn manager refuses to toss in the towel.

"Okay, let's say you aren't," Danny offers. "Let's say you're just Harry."

"Keep saying that," Harry says.

"How do you explain the girl?" Danny confronts him.

"You paid her," Harry quickly responds.

"How do you explain the 36 people who came from parts unknown to simultaneously and inexplicably come upon you?"

"You paid them," Harry doesn't hesitate.

"Look, under the worst of circumstances, you made 36 people with nothing to live for happy. Suddenly they've got an achievement under their belt. They found Jesus."

"Couldn't they just get reborn or sign up for a subscription to *AWAKE*?" Harry suggests.

"All I ask is that you entertain the idea. Is that asking too much, Harry? A lot of evidence is pointing your way, you know," Danny confides.

You have been weighing all the information. At first you weren't sure if this was a scam. Now you think that a philosophical point of significance has been reached. "This is no less legitimate than Milton Mallet's cook book," you think.

"Harry, do you believe in Christ?" you ask.

"Yes, of course," he answers.

"Do you have self-confidence?" you ask him.

"Well, yes. I'm my own person. I believe in myself," he says.

"Do you see the connection? You believe in Jesus and you believe in yourself. Isn't there some connection among the things you believe in? Aren't they all the sum of your faith?" you rattle, and Danny seems proud of your strength.

"I believe that the Cleveland Indians could win it all this year, too. Is there a Jesus connection there?" he stammers.

"They are on their way, too!" Danny comments with a smile.

"What I'm saying is that it's a matter of faith. There are millions of stories about people who could heal the sick," you continue.

"People who can bend forks and spoons with their minds!" Danny asserts.

"Look, either God and Jesus are in all of us or in none of us," you conclude.

Danny puts his forehead right up to Harry's chin, closes his eyes and lets a higher authority speak through him.

"You are the second coming of Christ. This word has been passed down through the multitudes. You don't have a choice," Danny says with great conviction.

"Come on, I mean, how extensive a search did you conduct?" Harry pleads.

"It has been recognized that there's more Jesus in you than in anyone in Toledo. And now we're going to work together to perfect it, to concentrate and focus it. We're going to put you through training, extensive training like an Olympic athlete to bring out your maximum Messiahship." Danny's short arms are shaking Harry from his shoulder blades, and Harry's cheeks are bouncing up and down like a rubber anxiety-relief doll.

"Fine, so where are we going with this line of thought?" Harry asks while Danny flattens Harry's face with the palms of his hands on each cheek.

"Wherever the Lord sends us," Danny answers softly.

"And I'm the Lord," Harry double-checks.

"For all practical purposes, you are Jesus. There's no arguing it," you answer.

"You are Jesus. He has returned in the body of you." Danny gets that business tone back in his voice.

"In the body of me," Harry repeats.

"Okay, well then, here is my first directive," Harry

commands as he points to a bottle of brand name vodka and grunts his need for it. Danny reaches over and grabs a cheap bottle you never heard of and slams it down in front of Harry.

"We have much to accomplish," Danny reminds him.

"Tie one on, buddy," you recommend.

Several days pass. Danny decided that Harry needed a few easy days for adjustment purposes, so he has converted the upstairs office into a sleeping room for the Messiah. The room is strewn with the debris from his every wish come true. Potato chip and fig bar wrappers, malted milk ball boxes.

Darryl has become Harry's groom and you are his right hand man. It occurs to you that you wouldn't mind ghost-writing a recipe book under Harry's name if this thing really catches on.

Harry wakes up on the third morning and has a raging headache from having hit the bar after-hours again. Danny has informed him that starting today, he's limited to non-alcoholic beer.

The phone was ringing nonstop. Danny arranged with the proprietor of Five Fingers to let him put call forwarding on their 1-900 sex line, and he put a small ad in the sports pages of the Toledo Blade promoting an exciting new call-in service named "1-900-Miracle" using the same number.

Pinky was in charge of answering the phone during the night, Zero during the day.

Nighttime calls were of a somewhat different nature than those they received during daylight.

"Call for a Miracle" Pinky would answer. "My finger is moving slowly down your back and I'm driving you crazy with its teasing circling motion," the gravely voice utters slowly and despicably.

"I'm about to touch your inner moistness," he continues as Pinky pops a huge bubble in the receiver and the caller groans and hangs up prematurely.

Soon, Harry will be handling these calls, once the miracle promotion starts catching on. But he needs a bit more preparation first. At the very least, he has to stop claiming that he's been kidnapped by "you fucking loon balls," and threatening to reveal that Talk of the Town is being used as a crash pad in a retail-only zone.

The sex calls are becoming so annoying that by the end of the day, Danny has installed an answering machine with its gentle message read by Father Mulroy:

Thank you for calling Danny's Talk of the Town. If you are calling for the Messiah please be advised that he already knows you are on the phone and he knows what you are in need of. Please stay on the line for as long as you would like him to pray for you. After five minutes, you qualify for a special half-price miracle minute package. Leave a message and he'll call you back in person.

"Not bad, huh?!" Danny said as the first caller held on for a good 7 minutes. "$2.99 a minute for air," he gloated.

"This is just a warm-up," he promises and he signals you to go outside and make sure everything is set for day one of Harry's training. He tells Darryl to clean up the mess and Darryl sneers at him. "When do I start doing my real thing?" he corners Danny. "Blowing things up, I mean, not cleaning," he drawls.

"Shut up Darryl," Danny suggests and Darryl starts picking up Harry's snack debris. He picks up a Little Debbie snack cake wrapper and can see Harry's tongue lick trail on the icing stuck to the top. Under his breath he says "If this is Jesus I'm Abraham Lincoln." Harry hears him and says "Darryl, could you get me some tangy taco dip next time out?"

Word has been getting out that some crazy religious thing is happening over at Danny's. You walk outside and, sure enough, a line of bizarre characters is already forming outside the door.

Father Mulroy and Father Pat come upstairs and say good morning to Harry. "Good morning Father," they refer to him as instructed. Danny thought it would be pushing the issue to get them to actually call him Jesus, and he didn't think it was appropriate to call the Messiah by his first name anyway.

You enter the chamber and Danny gives you the high sign. "Bring them on," he says, and you get the show on the road.

"Mr. Brian Stone," you announce each visitor like they're entering a debutante ball. "Deaf since birth and up shit creek with American Express," you finish the introduction.

"Heal him," Danny whispers to Harry. Harry looks at the deaf man and wonders why he has a walkman strapped to his belt. "Why not?" he says to himself as he stands up, clamps his hand to the guy's sweaty forehead and screams "Heal!!!"

"Hey, not so loud!!!" complains the visitor and everyone applauds Harry for having given the man the gift of hearing. "What about American Express?" he complains.

"Get a cash advance from your Visa, it always works for me. Keep about 10 of those cards rotating into each other and you can go on for years on interest only," Harry advises him.

"Thank you Jesus," the happy man tells Harry as he is yanked out of the room by Zeke.

"Ms. Karen Pinkton," you announce. "Permanently infertile."

"I wouldn't mind healing this one in private," Harry giggles softly to Danny. "Heal her," Danny instructs.

"Heal!!!!" Harry tosses his hand at her forehead, but she ducks and he rams it into the picture of Cher mounted on the wall. It falls to the floor and the glass breaks in to a thousand pieces.

"I feel, I feel – I feel all tingly!" Ms. Pinkton hugs her body all over. "Go to your honey," Harry advises her and she runs out the door ready to give that in-fertility a run for its money.

A variety of people inflicted with one handicap after another show up throughout the day. Blind, deaf, coughing, wheezing, dying. They enter in pain and agony, and they leave completely cured, happy as larks.

A number of unplanned visitors show up and you try to be hospitable although you cannot let them in at this time.

Some are truly on their last legs. One lady wanted a small miracle. "I'm willing to wear eyeglasses, but could he arrange for me not to need bifocals?" she asked.

The day ends when Zeke walks up the stairs care-fully escorting two blind old men. You can tell they were blind because they have canes. When Father Mulroy asks if he can help them, one of them an-swers "Don't think so. Nice shine on them shoes," to which Darryl says, "Thanks. It's about time I got some respect over here."

"Harry, there are two people here who need your help," says Danny as he and Zeke lead the two blind men to his side. Harry is sucking on a frozen plastic wrapped stick of grape punch.

"Give it a chance, Harry, give it a chance," Danny urges him.

"We've been blind since birth," says one of them.

"I have never seen my daughter's smile, my son's curve ball or my wife's erect nipples," says the other.

"Pray for us, Jesus!"

"Pray for a miracle Harry," Danny whispers in Harry's ear.

Harry notices that one of the blind men has a folded up racing form in his jacket pocket, but Danny quickly notes, "This man has never worn a pair of matching socks in his lifetime."

"Okay, gentlemen, I'm going to sort of swat you on the foreheads and you're going to probably fall over in a stupor. Is this okay with both of you?" Harry asks the two.

"No," Danny says to Harry. "Let's start getting a respectable action going here," he says out loud, but no one seems the least bit curious, except for Harry who thinks he's been doing quite well at this healing thing.

"You ever seen the Mighty Hans at the wrestling matches?" Danny asks him.

"Of course," Harry answers.

"Toss a 'mighty claw' at them. A Brain Claw," Danny explains.

"This was a hold invented by Jesus?" Harry asked.

"It was invented by Mighty Hans, but it's a good visual, now let's try it. You just splay your hand out like a big stiff spider," Danny helps Harry form his right hand in proper healing fashion.

"Then you grab the claw's wrist with your other hand and try to hold it back from striking. But the claw now has a mind of it's own and says 'I gotta do what I gotta do' and it strikes!" he slams Harry's mighty claw to the head of Father Pat. "Now clamp on and start shuddering!" Danny orders.

Father Pat's feeble, lanky body is shaking so hard, Queen Isadora is rattling like a set of dice in her round plastic carrying case. "Is this altogether necessary?!" she screeches, but as usual, no one cares what an ant has to say.

"That's it, you've got it, now show us some serious healing," Danny roots Harry on as he aims him at the blind men.

Harry attaches his mighty claw to the first blind man's forehead and starts shaking it from his elbow down like a vibrator until the man legitimately topples over in to the waiting arms of Zeke who lets him down gently.

"You forgot to say 'Heal.'" Danny reminds him.

"Oh. Heal!" Harry yells to the figure now flat on his back on the floor.

"It would be good if you had a bit of a southern twang while you're at it," he adds.

"Heal them Lord!" Harry blurts at the floor.

"Now, quick, slam a claw at the other one." Danny aims Harry at Blind Man #2, who falls to the ground at first touch of Harry's quivering hand.

Immediately, both men are stirring, their eyes pulsating. And they each open their eyes and look around.

"I can see!" says the first.

"It's a miracle. Thank you Jesus," says the other.

As they leave, you notice that Zeke tucks a small envelope into each of their pockets.

You can hear them talking loudly enough for everyone to hear.

"He is absolutely Jesus Christ, wouldn't you say, Horace?" says one to the other.

"No question about it. Only Jesus could give the gift of sight," answers the other.

"I agree. And by the way, you are ugly!" teases the first.

"What do you say, Harry?" Danny asks.

"It's a miracle, that's for sure," Father Mulroy adds.

"It's hog slop," Harry responds. "If those two guys are blind, then I'm Mona Lisa," he proclaims.

"Well, they aren't blind any more! That's the point!" Danny teases gleefully.

"Don't fight it, Harry," you suggest to him as you close the doors after a good day of hard-working healing.

"Being a savior is not a bad career move for you at this point in your life," Danny notes.

Danny takes off, leaving you and Darryl to tend to

the Lord your God with whatever morsels which will constitute his ambrosia for this evening.

"Give me neither poverty nor riches; feed me with food convenient for me," Harry recites to you. He's been spoon-fed Bible quotations for several days by Father Mulroy and he's starting to sound pretty authoritative.

"Who said that?" you ask.

"Well, I did, I guess you'd say!" he laughs. "Providence 30, verse 8," he gloats, privately thinking that he always did feel secretly special, and maybe he is the one and only. After all, someone has to be.

Meanwhile, Danny has tracked down the embroidery machine over in the police custody warehouse and he is on the phone arranging to meet with Father Pat and Bishop Flagg to discuss terms of settlement.

Chapter Thirty Four

Danny is seated on a white chair in front of a blue background as the red light starts blinking on the camera aimed at him. He sneaks a look in the studio monitor and is confused by how it looks like he's sitting on a rooftop overlooking the skyline of downtown Cleveland, the new Gateway ballpark's lights forming a nice halo around his bald little head.

"Mr. DeMarco, are you going to sit here today and tell the world that Jesus Christ has returned to this life, and he's living in Toledo, Ohio on the second floor of a common bar?" the news reporter asks Danny, who is scooching the knot on his red tie so it's centered on the matching red shirt which ties in so nicely with the red silk handkerchief jammed in to his breast pocket.

"He has good taste," Danny jokes. Holding the news conference in Cleveland was a great idea because nobody in Toledo would even entertain the notion that something of importance happened in their own town. Clevelanders sort of viewed Toledo as a distant suburb, anyway, and they would embrace any major Toledo achievement as their own.

"Mr. DeMarco, when can we see him?" a shapely anchorwoman with a name tag that says "Candy Lovejoy, TV7-Sports," is reading her question off a cue card.

"Ms. Lovejoy, how can anyone answer that? We're not talking about a photo opportunity with the President. This is the Lord our God!" Danny answers devoutly and then winks at her, which she responds to with a gag reflex.

"How can he prove he's really the Messiah?" asks the self-assured newsman with the gray off-kilter hair piece and a pair of glasses with no lenses in them.

"What do you want, a miracle?" Danny laughs again. He's basking in the attention at the live news interview he arranged by calling the station that had the cutest weatherman and pretending to be his own public relations agent.

You and the crew are all watching Danny on the TV sets at Danny's. The Talk of the Town has now been fully converted to "The Second Coming Official Headquarters" as evidenced by the huge blue and red banner draped from its rooftop. Every now and then, the wind blows up big enough so you can read a bit of the back of the banner, which says something about "More mint flavor in every manly chew."

For the last two days, Harry has been spoon-fed a regular diet of people who can't walk, who can't see, who can't move, who can't think. He concentrates, slams their foreheads, and each and every one is healed right then and there. On the spot.

"Do you believe it now, Harry?" Danny would never stop asking.

"I don't feel like Jesus Christ. I feel just like me," Harry would answer wearily.

"If you weren't Jesus Christ, you'd think you were Him. Don't you see, Jesus would never want to think He was Himself," Danny would explain.

"Listen, Harry, he's right," helps Father Mulroy. "In your own words, right from the great book, listen: Whoever shall exalt himself shall be abased; and he that shall humble himself shall be exalted.

Harry liked that sentiment, and he has seen his powers do an awful lot of good over the last few days, his natural instincts bringing a great deal of humility to the picture.

"Maybe I'm the manifestation of Jesus, which is not all that bad," he thinks to himself. He recalls that he always did have a very good touch with his ants. Well, there were a few who would from time to time just topple over dead, but he attributed that to a severe case of ant PMS which no one, Jesus included, has ever overcome.

Back at the news conference, the lights behind Danny go out, the Indians beat Toronto 4-1 and are finally in the playoffs. The rich people, not satisfied to have shut out the regular fan from sitting anywhere near the playing field, now want to buy the rights to sit on the actual bases, and, of course, have them named after them.

It was nice of smokers to cough up most of the

cost of building the place, especially considering they aren't allowed to light up inside it.

"Look, when he's ready, you'll meet him and believe me, you'll know it's him. I've seen him already cure the blind. I've seen him already make a lame person walk. He doesn't even know his own powers. He is so humble, he denies his own divinity. Just be patient, folks. He'll be glad to talk to each and every one of you." Danny is in heaven.

"I am going to set up a tribunal. Members of the Church. Members of the community. People who have joined him. I want all the world to judge for themselves," Danny promises at the close of the news segment.

"Well, there you have it, the second coming – oh, and Mr. DeMarco, how does your Messiah explain that when he was to return, there would be an apocalypse?" asks the weather lady who has accidentally stepped in front of the blue screen and appears to be suspended in mid air over Cleveland's Public Square.

"Well, you'll have to ask him. Maybe after 2000 years he's rethought a few of those less productive ideas," answers Danny.

Danny DeMarco. Man of God. Advance man for Jesus.

Talk about miracles!

Everyone seems very happy. Danny is laughing.

211

The news people are salivating. It's such a stagger-ing opportunity, nobody wants to be the first to set a tone to it. Is this funny? Is it quirky? Is it dangerous?

Or, in the best of all cases, is it actually the Sec-ond Coming?

Frannie is distracted from the newscast by a blunt feeling in her head. She puts her hands to her temples and rubs them hard with her knuckles. She is breathing in short little bursts, the next quicker than the last, the one after that even sooner.

"Harry, what have they done to Harry?!!!" she gasps. This is becoming serious. Her brother. Danny taking advantage. Harry falling for it. Life is upsetting. The earth is turning and she is sticking out of its surface spinning like a pair of dungarees in the Laundromat. Harry Jesus. Jesus Harry. Impossible. CBS news. Channel 7. Harry her brother. Danny what are you doing...she is breathing out so quickly, she's unable to breath in and...

...Frannie seems to tip a bit to each side before she collapses to the ground, her head fortunately landing on Zeke's soft leather shoes, unfortunately rolling off them and slamming into the foot of the bar stool.

Harry is upstairs catching some tunes on his new Sony discman, so he doesn't hear any of this.

"Call EMS," Zeke screams to the heavens.

"Jesus Christ!" you respond as you leap for the phone and dial 911.

Father Mulroy runs upstairs to Harry's room and bangs on the door. Harry's head is wrapped in stereo headphones, and he's pounding his feet to "Love Me Two Times Babe."

In moments, an ambulance arrives and whisks Frannie to the hospital.

You're secretly glad that Harry didn't know what was going on. This was not a time when such a god would choose to be tested.

Father Pat is reading Psalms to the Uncle Milton
Ant Farm, while lounging about the Church study
wearing his charter member "Second Coming" T-
Shirt. Queen Isadora is in her own special quarters,
limping around, constantly angry that she can't get
that leg going properly, and severely frustrated that
all those young studs are separated from her by two
panes of plastic.

All of the pew people are over at Danny's where
they have become specialists in crowd control, constantly regulating the flow of the miserable who are
drawn to Harry's legendary healing power.

The report on Frannie is, of course, weird from
Danny's point-of-view. "Hyperventilation due to hys-
teria!" he mimicked the doctor when they finally
bothered reporting her condition to everyone waiting.

"What is this, a cartoon disease??? Is there a reporter from *MAD Magazine* handling this???" he
mouthed off to the doctor.

"It's not that rare," the physician calmly said to
Danny.

"A complex migraine syndrome combined with a
hysterical reaction to anything in her environment
could result in hyperventilation. Her carbon dioxide
level fell so low, she passed out. Her nervous system
became destabilized," he explained.

"You're telling me that Frannie is in the hospital

because something surprised her," Danny translates.

"Actually, she's in her condition because of the concussion she suffered when she fell to the floor," the doctor revealed.

"What condition is this?" Danny asked.

"She's been in a coma since she arrived. We don't know how it's affected her. We would expect her to come out of it soon. We're watching her carefully," he concluded as Danny took Harry to her room where Harry revealed the child in him, confused but not alarmed, she looked so pleasantly asleep.

"Heal, Frannie," he said softly as he kissed her forehead good-bye. "I'm sure she'll be fine," Danny assured him as they left.

A week later and Danny has replaced the chintzy screen doors with oversized old oak. Harry is nervous about his sister, but Danny reports that this is just the expected thing that happens when someone is tired and gets bumped on the head. "She'll be out of it any time now," Danny had reassured Harry.

"Maybe she needs an operation, Danny. She's been out for so long!" Harry complained.

"You've saved dozens of people from much bigger problems. When you have a moment, concentrate on Frannie. Healing her will be no problem," Danny suggested.

"I have to see her again," Harry insisted.

"Taking you outside right now is a security risk," Danny told him. "And your sister doesn't need that kind of pressure," he added.

Danny has been thinking overtime, envisioning a spectacular event, the crowning hour of civilization, the return of Jesus in a great venue possibly extended even further with pay-per-view.

"The Second Coming," he loves whispering those words to himself. "Jesus Christ, live and in person, recreating his greatest miracles of all time."

"I love this life," Danny howls to the skies. Father Pat comes to Danny's side and mentions that "Harry is hungry," and that they've run out of petty cash for snacks.

"He demands something to eat," Father Pat repeats.

"Tell him to create something!" Danny proclaims.

The clunky, creaky wooden door slams open. Three Priests clad in solid black enter and part the doors for two higher-presence Priests clad in solid white.

"Fathers," the surprised Father Pat quietly greets his two visitors.

"Bishop Flagg, Bishop Hutt, I can't recall having so many Bishops grace my presence," he shares.

"What is this?" Bishop Flagg points to the Second Coming T-Shirt.

"A souvenir. Say, how are those Pope shirts selling? I hear they're all the rage," Danny snickers.

"Father, are you participating in this sham?" Bishop Hutt addresses Father Pat who is aging before your eyes.

"What's one sham over another?" he answers.

"They're selling these?" Bishop Flagg asks the Father as he tries to judge the stitch count of the cotton-polyester blend.

"They couldn't get in to production. You took their equipment," Father Pat answers matter-of-factly.

"We want to meet him." "Immediately," they both demand.

"Who?" asks the slow moving Father.

"You know exactly who, Father, and I might add,

never let me see you in such a blasphemous garb again. In addition to it being completely sinful, it is also clearly a willful violation of our intellectual property rights. We can hold you culpable!!!" Bishop Hutt attacks him as the Father reaches in to his pocket and pulls Isadora out, her still trying to stretch that gimp leg in to proper operation. She looks toward Bishop Hutt and giggles at she notices that his beeper is strapped around a fake crocodile belt.

"You want to meet Harry?" the Father asks.

"Father, perhaps you do not realize the severity of this situation." Bishop Flagg becomes a bit warmer.

"Well, Fathers, haven't we been praying for this moment forever?" Father Pat responds softly. "Why are you so surprised at the possibility that our prayers were actually answered?" he adds.

Father Mulroy sticks his head around the corner and adds "Something's fishy when the rain man doesn't carry an umbrella."

Everyone looks at him in complete confusion, so he explains "Your first instinct when your greatest dream comes true is that it must be false. Did you ever actually believe that Jesus would be returning if you are so shocked that he might have really done it?" he continues.

You promise to set up a meeting and you wish the holy men well. As they leave, you note that one of

219

the men in black appears to be wearing a shoulder harness.

Harry has cured hundreds. He's to the point now that he doesn't even have to toss brain claws at them, in fact, he can service several at a time. The line goes on forever, and frankly, both you and he are getting bored.

"I think I'm ready to move on to bigger and better miracles," Harry says one day.

"Your day appears to be coming," you answer as you unfold Danny's newest creation, a T-Shirt vest that says "Meet Me At The Second Coming." Danny figures on getting all the town's most shapely girls to wear them next Saturday during the special "Day Of Jesus" celebration that had been planned for months before Harry arrived.

"It's in commemoration of you, Harry," you hold the shirt up to your chest and laugh at how little of it the shirt covers.

"You know, you've healed an awful lot of people, Harry. Do you think it could possibly be true?" you ask.

"How would I know?" he answers.

"I haven't healed Frannie," he reminds you.

"They're doing an MRI in a few days. That'll give us the straight story," you tell him.

"I'm going to see her," he demands.

"After the test," you compromise.

"We need to plan the crowd control. People want to meet you," you tell him. The phone does ring off the hook, and there's a whole crew of people who call you constantly because you know him. Not a bad situation.

"Look, Al, let's suppose I am the Messiah. I don't have any recollection of anything about a first life. I don't remember being killed. I never went to Temple. I don't want to go to Church. I don't even know if I believe in God," he confides.

"Well, isn't it true that the first time around, you felt the same way?" you ask.

"I think I believed in God," Harry answers.

"Well, the son is always the last one to see the greatness in his father," you offer. "To all those people you've healed, you are the Son of God, like it or not."

"You say this, not me. I never even read about it," Harry closes the conversation just as the door bangs open and Father Pat appears. He looks frantic as he holds the medicine vial out to Harry.

"Isadora can't walk. You must save her!" he exclaims.

The Queen takes one look at Harry and wants to wring his neck for entrusting her to this dunderhead.

"Heal her," you say. "You've got to be able to cure an ant, for God's sake," you add.

Harry takes the vial in hand and with a simple shrug of his shoulders, puckers up his lips toward

the vial and pokes his little finger at it as he says
"Heal."

Isadora is about ready to scream. "I don't need
Jesus! I need an orthopedist!!" she howls.

The vial slips a little as Harry hands it back to the
Father, and Isadora suffers yet another body blow.
"And I want a good lawyer too, damn it!" she bel-
lows.

Father Pat drops the vial carefully in his pocket
and walks out backwards, eternally thankful for the
great favor from the King of Kings. The Queen
bides her time. She's sure her moment will come
when these peasants will appreciate her significance
in life.

Chapter Thirty Nine

Frannie has remained in a coma for two weeks. Danny marches to the hospital to meet with the surgeon. Harry has been quite distracted and has accepted that this simply proves how badly she needed a break and some quiet time.

"We've done a scan, we've done three, they all come up the same. She must have surgery," the doctor explains to Danny.

"It's critical. We can't take a chance on the clot receding on its own," he continues.

"Look, this is my girlfriend, and we don't believe in fancy cure-alls. What if she just waits it out?" Danny asks.

"It would take a miracle under those circumstances," answers the surgeon.

"I never heard of anybody operating on a dizzy spell!" Danny argues.

"Sir, your girlfriend has a blood clot very close to her brain and it is compressing the organ. We don't know if it has stopped bleeding. We need to remove it," the doctor tries to be calm.

"Just tell me this, can it go away on its own?" Danny asks.

"It can, but you can't rely on this. She could die at any second, and the risk of surgery is well within reason."

"Whose reason?" Danny confronts him.

"Acceptable medical tolerances," the surgeon eyes

him back.

"Yeah, well, has a day ever gone by when someone hasn't died in here?" Danny questions him.

"People die every day. That's what people do at the end of their lives!" the doctor storms back.

"Well, I can't tolerate professionals who have failure built into their procedures," Danny beams, turns around and walks away.

"And you shouldn't be so skeptical about miracles," Danny turns around and reminds him. "People don't tend to die from them, either," he laughs and heads to the exit as the doctor walks to the nurse's stand and exclaims, "Jesus freak!"

Danny didn't want to distract Harry with worrying about his sister, but even Danny understood the laws of basic decency.

"She's going to be just fine," he explains. "It's still that headache thing, probably too much estrogen running through her veins," he adds.

"What do the doctors say?" Harry asks.

"They say she's half way home already," says Danny.

"Why don't you come down to the hospital and give her one more healing session. I think that's all she really needs," Danny suggests. "Personal healing."

Danny has avoided returning Harry to the hospital because he didn't want to create a scene. Mostly, he doesn't want Harry to lose faith in his own special powers.

Danny dresses Harry up in an old cook's uniform he once bought when he was thinking of turning the place in to a Yuppie bistro. They take a taxi to the hospital, just the two of them, and there the brother and the lover stand silently over Frannie, the silly, warm caboose, the loving, caring friend, and if there will ever be a moment of honesty between them, this is the time.

"Harry, give her all you've got," Danny instructs him. "It's in your heart and soul and you can cure her. Touch her head and she will heal."

"If you say so, Danny," and Harry gives the unconscious Frannie his best gentle brain claw and his most optimistic utterance. "HEAL!!!! Heal Frannie!!!!" but she doesn't stir.

"It probably takes more time to kick in when they're already knocked out," explains Danny.

The time has come to expand, to capitalize on an equity called Harry. Harry has been a good Joe. You don't know if he completely believes that he is the Messiah, but he's enjoying the healing process. He's like the kid who thinks he can fly, knowing full-well, most of the time, that he can't.

But for that moment when he's standing on the edge of his bed, arms out front, ready to take his maiden voyage, his mind fully believes it's ready to go into orbit.

The state of suspended disbelief is a concept you've been confronted with often lately. You wonder whether or not this state of being is when we're closest to being one with God.

Somehow, and you can't believe it's a 100% bought and paid for illusion, people seem to heal when Harry does his thing. And the more faith Harry has in his abilities, the more completely they seem to be affected.

It's like the old story you had once read about Hans the Clever Horse. Hans' trainer supposedly taught the horse how to add, subtract, even multiply and divide. The trainer would ask "Hans, how much is 24 divided by 6?" and he would stand there excited as Hans would tap out the answer, to the trainer's sheer delight.

It turned out that Hans had no idea how to count, but he could detect when his owner was happy. The trainer would reveal his satisfaction when the horse had tapped out the right number, and sensing that delight, the horse would stop tapping!

Harry too, does not know for sure how he heals people, just that he knows how people behave when they think the healing has kicked in, and he has learned how to get them to feel that way.

He's almost at the point of being out of control, because every time he's introduced to anyone, his first impulse is to toss his healing hand at their forehead.

Just this morning when Harry came downstairs for his cup of coffee and frozen waffle, Ralph the liqueur salesman walked in carrying a new promotional table tent.

"We're out of that business, Ralph. We're in to religion now," barked Danny.

"Just in case that doesn't work out, there's always a need for a good stiff drink, Danny," the elderly, cordial fellow reminded him.

"Early customer?" said Ralph as he looked at Harry swallowing the waffle in one huge bite.

"This is Harry. Harry, meet Ralph," Danny introduced them without looking up from the media plan which his new ad agency, Opinion Concepts, had mailed him that morning.

"Used to eat breakfast, but my ulcer just won't accept food at this time of morning anymore," Ralph complained.

Like Pavlov's dog, Harry robotically turned to the man, walked directly over to him, slammed his brain with his practiced claw and screamed "Heal!!!" Ralph grabbed his table tent package, his eyes bugging out at Harry, and ran for the door. Harry, who dropped half the waffle from his mouth during the process, wondered why the guy didn't fall to the ground as people usually do.

"Maybe you could use a second treatment," he called to Ralph who is now well outside the door.

Harry opened the door and yelled to the guy walking quickly down the street. "These things usually work the first time. I'm really sorry!"

Point being, Harry has learned to enjoy this. He feels deeply inadequate when his subjects fail to topple over in ecstasy at the climax of his actions. He doesn't even concern himself with whether or not they are cured of anything.

Your thinking is that it really doesn't matter whether or not anyone is actually, permanently healed. And, for that matter, you're learning to believe that the act of thinking one is healed is the essential part of the actual healing. Haven't many people laughed at life's punishments and beaten the odds because they refused to believe in their bad luck?

You believe that you can choose your own fate, and that you can reject a bad one. Your mind can be conditioned to be a place where negative influences cannot penetrate.

Danny probably understood this all along, which is why he has no qualms about popularizing the idea. That's why he's meeting with Clark Daniger at Opinion Concepts in Cleveland this afternoon. They attracted his attention due to their recent success as the promoters of the "Tough Guy Championships," a particularly exciting event where punks off the street competed in no-holds-barred fist fights on stage.

You're very excited that he invited you to join the meeting. "I don't want them to think they're dealing with small potatoes. Tell them you're the corresponding secretary or something," he advised you.

"Or the treasurer, whatever," Danny isn't your typical management role model.

"Mr. DeMarco, we don't give a rat's ass whether he's Jesus or a man from mars. Theater is theater, know what I mean?" laughs the tall, slightly balding ad guy, who works to make sure his creative side shows by letting the hair surrounding his baldness grow to great lengths, all curled up like a hedge of unkempt evergreens.

"That's very nice, Clark," coughs Danny as Clark blows a smoke ring in the air that loops its way around Danny's head.

"The media plan, strategically speaking, balances reach and frequency just where we like to see it. Basically, when we combine trade with cash, we can reach every man and woman from Detroit to Buffalo within budget," Clark promises.

"Great. Now let's talk about terms," says Danny.

"First, the creative," slurps Clark who can't wait to uncover the big board sitting on the easel which is just like the one Danny used in his first Pope presentation to Father Pat.

"The creative? Creative is a thing? I thought it was an adjective or an adverb. Creative art. Creative person. Here you call it The Creative, like it's holy?" complains Danny.

"Looks like we're in the same business, pretty much, huh?!!!" the ad guy chortles and slaps Danny on his back.

"What if the creative isn't really creative, then

what do you call it?" you ask.

"Well, then I guess we'd have to call it – a bunch of shit!!!" he laughs. "But we know what we're doing here. Let me show you." And Clark gets up and calls in his assistant, a shapely young woman with extraordinarily long earlobes. "Eunice, give me a hand here, will you?" and she struts up along side the artwork, and together they lift the flap.

"We call this the moment of truth," Clark says with great reverence.

You look at the artwork. You look at Danny. Danny walks up to it and stares at it closely. He huffs and puffs. Clark thinks no one is looking as he pats Eunice's rear end and she responds with a secret smile.

"What do you think?" Clark asks.

"It's brilliant," says the star-struck Danny.

"And you?" he challenges.

"You misspelled Christ," you note.

"This is just a rough. Eunice, doesn't that spellcheck thing on your computer know how to spell Jesus Christ, for God's sake!!!" and he laughs again.

"The Second Coming," Danny whispers. "The Greatest Miracles of all Time, Live and In Person."

The artwork has a picture of Harry in a white robe standing in the middle of a huge puddle surrounded by throngs of beseeching fans stacked up on stadium seats.

"July 4. Toledo Mud Hen's Stadium," Danny reads.

"We think the concept is right on target, Mr. De-Marco.

"Where's the ad copy?" Danny asks.

"If you approve all of this, we'll have the final copy to you by tomorrow," answers Eunice, who you could swear has been sneaking looks at you.

"We need a killer headline," Danny tells them. "Like for a big movie," chimes Clark.

You take a chance and make eye contact with Eunice, who immediately pulverizes you by returning a sneer, but it doesn't bother you because you figure that she was just tricked into revealing her low class background.

She yanks her skirt to let you know the party's over.

"You'll have the whole package in your hands for approval tomorrow," Clark promises.

"What about credit terms?" Danny gets back in his seat, ready to talk turkey.

"We get billed by the media thirty days after the stuff airs, and you pay us thirty days after that," answers Clark. He leans in and drops his voice down low and adds, "You play your cards right and you can practically get the media to finance your whole ad program."

"We can go with that," says Danny.

"But they're bandits. They'll charge whatever they can get away with. That's why you need us," Clark reminds him.

"Yeah, you're even bigger bandits," Danny laughs as they shake hands to call it a day.

"This will translate on TV and radio like dynamite," Clark continues as they walk through the mirrored, shag-rugged office that is so far out of date, it's back in fashion.

"We've got it all figured out. Press kits that look like Holy Bibles. The TV commercial takes the Moses thing in to another generation," Clark closes. "You'll have it first thing in the morning," Eunice tells Danny, and then with a surprise smile at you she says, "I'll bring it all by myself."

"You know, if you guys really come through, I think I could get Harry to make you disciples or saints, whatever you'd like," Danny offers.

"If we had been there the first time around, Danny, every person on earth would be a Christian today," Clark says with feigned humility.

Word got out that Harry curing people by the box-car. Of course, there had been many self-proclaimed healers and prophets surfacing from time to time, but this was different.

Others have claimed to be the Messiah, but no one ever before had T-Shirts and sweatshirts celebrating their arrival, while simultaneously denying their own divinity. Prophets and false gods rarely reveal such personality conflicts.

The TV, radio and all the press hit just like Clark had promised. Toledo was buzzing with excitement. No one could remember tickets selling for anything this quickly.

Father Mulroy found this completely delightful, his own personal logic run amok, a certain spiritual giggling permeating his character.

"How can you enjoy such a stunt?" you ask, at the same time asking yourself "What's an honest and decent fellow like me doing in this bizarre charade?"

Both questions share an answer. If life could look at itself, of course it would laugh. We are so afraid of not knowing why we are here.

The evidence of people's need to believe and their willingness to be kindly with the standards they apply in that matter, was building hourly. The Second Coming was going to be a big moneymaker. There was the slight problem of funding the special effects, but Danny seemed to feel that this could be handled.

You stumble through each day and night devouring this experience, oddly enchanted that you've become part of the madness and that you don't find it the least bit deceitful.

So far, it's fairly harmless, not much more significant than the Madam Zaza or Brother Love characters who advertise in the local paper promising miracles and cures, or for an extra few dollars, the blessed number of the week.

Except Danny has a knack. He understands that the media will make this whole thing grow because they need to nurture it so it will become a great big story. He knows how they like to run stories through carefully choreographed cycles, from a little discovery to a big revelation, to a heroic climax followed by complete discreditation of the entire thing.

The Second Coming was made to order.

And in walks Eunice wearing an enormous fake rabbit fur coat. "I'm an animal activist," she teases you. "Well, that's convenient, because I'm an animal and..." you risk making a complete fool of yourself but this may be just the woman for you and you know how much women like wise guys.

She gives you this scan from your knees to your navel and comments accurately, "Looks like I've activated you, too."

Danny breaks up the budding romance. "I need the stuff now. My financial people are waiting on me," he says urgently as Eunice rips open the package and sets everything up on the bar.

"First, the ad and poster, which are the driving forces of the whole campaign," says Eunice very professionally. You are trying to detect if she is wearing any underwear, and her tight black stretch pants are providing no evidence that anything other than them is separating you from her intimacy.

Danny reads the colorful poster out loud with great drama.

"2000 Years Ago He Walked On Water. That Was Just Practice. Experience The Miracle of The Second Coming." Danny looks to the heavens when he's done and says "Thank you Lord."

"You're welcome," says Eunice. She looks at you and sneers again. You decide that you actually do like neurotic women, and you find it appealing that this one makes no effort to hide her condition.

"Take a look at the TV copy," Eunice tells Danny as she pats her behind lightly, and you are sure she's inviting you to study it.

Danny reads down the video side of the script, which describes Moses coming down the mountain carrying a huge stone tablet containing each of the ten commandments. The stone is struck by lightning. The commandments are obliterated, replaced by copy that reads: 11th Commandment. See The Second Coming.

"I love it!" Danny screeches. "It's perfect. Gotta run," and he dashes out the door with all the advertising material, leaving Eunice there to clarify her intentions with you.

"Would you like to see a movie some time?" you ask her.

"With who?" she answers.

"Well, I like movies," you respond nervously.

"I don't go out with guys like you," she scoffs.

"Why not?"

"Sex maniacs," she gives you twice the usual sneer, puts her fake fur on and leaves, ostensibly disgusted with you, but no one's going to tell you her hips normally swing to that extent if she isn't trying to communicate an attraction.

Danny is very positive about his meeting. He bursts in the door of the Holiday Inn's conference ballroom where there's a single table in the middle with two people seated there in the dark. One of them is wearing a plastic mask with a huge nose and giant bushy eyebrows. The other one has ace bandages wrapped around each leg.

"It's outstanding!" says the disguised wealthiest motherfucker in Argentina. Herb Spritz, himself, has returned to Toledo, apparently at great risk, just because Dolores Irons told him it was the investment opportunity of his lifetime.

"If he isn't Jesus by some chance, the real Jesus is definitely going to be out to get you," Herb laughs.

"You're going to need some protection," Dolores advises very seriously, and Danny says he'll take it under advisement.

"Consider your investment an act of good faith," Danny suggests. Herb is twiddling with his gold H's and S's linked together around his neck. Dolores is smacking away at a calculator even though no numbers have been discussed.

"I'm a Jew, Danny," Herb sighs.

"So was Jesus," Danny reminds him.

"And Harry is a Jew too?" Herb perks up.

"All Harry knows is that he's Jesus. We've spared him the details," Danny laughs and adds "He does not believe that he is Jesus, but I'm telling you that this is something we have going for us. It reeks of sincerity," explains Danny.

"Yes, but who would believe it?" asks Herb.

"Everyone, because the healing part is easy, and with a little capital, the miracle part is no big shakes either. I'm not casting any stones, but even way back then it wouldn't have taken a Houdini to double up on some loaves of bread," says Danny.

"What's the nut?" Dolores Irons gets to the point.

"Yes, how much?" echoes Herb.

"A hundred grand and we've got a show," Danny quickly responds. "Three for the stadium, nothing for the labor cause everyone thinks it's a holy thing, and forty or so for the special effects," Danny is serious and deliberate. "The rest is going into advertising, which is already on the air but I've got to pay them immediately." Danny continues as he laughs inside that he just got a free float of $57,000 to do with as he pleases until media settlement day.

"And the profit?" asks Dolores.

"Twenty three thousand in the seats, five thousand on the field, average ticket a C-note –"

"A hundred dollars for a show in the Mud Hens Stadium?" Herb says in disbelief.

"We're talking about Jesus Christ here! It could be a thousand dollars and we'd fill the joint!" Danny exclaims.

"At a hundred dollars a pop, a sell out delivers

$280,000, that's a $180,000 profit, and then?" Dolores plows ahead.

"And that's just a little test marketing. Then we take the act to serious places where the sky's the limit!" Danny concludes.

"We need the Church behind us," Herb Spritz deduces. "I don't know that this can fly with just Jewish backing. We need the Church involved in some way, in any way. I mean, after all, he's their founder!" he adds.

"We've got a priest," says Danny.

"We need someone higher. What's higher than a priest?" he asks both of them.

"A Bishop is higher than a priest," says Dolores Irons.

"I can't deliver a Bishop. But we may be able to get them to participate," says Danny.

"I don't care if they endorse it. Even if they come out against it, they'll give us some credibility," says Herb.

"When Jesus comes back, doesn't that pretty much call it a ball game for Christianity?" he asks Dolores, who grunts and reaches down to snap at the bandages around her left calf.

"There are two Bishops who want to meet him. And what comes of that is going to be as close to proof positive as there could be. They might not agree, but the public will," explains Danny.

Herb looks to Dolores, she pounds her fist on the table to signify her blessing and Herb says, "You get him through a session with a certified Bishop or two, and you've got a deal."

Television has hit. The posters are everywhere. Harry is all the Jesus one could ever have hoped for. He can't deny it any longer. Whoever and whatever Jesus is, he fits the bill. Maybe there's something to it. In fact, lately you've detected a bit of arrogance in Harry.

"I don't like how I look. I just don't feel holy today," he said as he woke up this important morning.

"You look like always, Harry. You look like Harry," you tried to soothe him.

"Well, that's not good enough, Al. I'm not just Harry anymore. In fact, I've been meaning to talk to you about that," he became very serious.

"Yes?" you answered.

"I can feel my significance," he eyed you.

"That's fine, Harry," you said. "But I wouldn't let it go to my head. You have a world outside of Toledo to convince," you added.

"People call me 'Heavenly Father' and, Al, you can see the tears in their eyes when they just look at me." Harry was agog with himself.

"Maybe you make them sad, Harry," you replied.

"Maybe you make them feel disappointed that even the Messiah isn't all he is cracked up to be. It's like London, Harry. You get off the plane, glance around at everything trying to look like it's American and you can't help but note that even London isn't what London's supposed to be any more. Nothing lives up to its image. You have to enjoy something for it's image, not for its reality. Actually, the Messiah probably wasn't ever intended to be met first hand, and London wasn't meant to be visited."

"I make them shudder," he stated flatly.

There's only so long one can see magic happening around him without being convinced he's a magician. It is perfectly natural to develop an ego about one's abilities, but you are afraid that Harry is beginning to define himself by standards that no mortal can live up to.

"I'd go slow on this line of thought," you suggested.

You can't deny that Harry the Heavenly Father's powers are becoming limitless. But you can't forget that Frannie has not stirred despite having had Harry's hands laid on her several times now. The last time Harry visited, he was so certain that he could heal her that he confronted the doctor who had been demanding the brother approve surgery.

"Doctor, heal thyself," said Harry as he rose to his feet and walked slowly to the door, his hands cupped beneath his chin.

"This is absolutely criminal!" the doctor muttered.

"Doctor, if you're looking for wrongdoing, how about all the doctors she saw before this happened?" cautioned Danny.

"She is not going to live," the doctor flatly stated.

"Don't underestimate the power of faith, doctor," Danny reminded him.

"Okay, well you tell your Jesus over there that when he's ready to give up on his miracle and face the music, I hope it isn't too late for us to save her," the doctor concluded.

Harry stuck his head back in the room and called to Danny.

"I just healed a woman with emphysema, Danny," he proudly proclaimed.

Danny smirked at the doctor and followed Harry out. "So heal your sister, smart guy," Danny muttered. "I did," Harry answered proudly. "Same as the others. It's a mysterious ability, Danny, and I appreciate that you helped me discover it," he said somberly.

The doctor followed them, giving a seriously curious glance at the nurse standing by the supposedly healed patient's room.

"He saw my cigarette pack and threw it in the wastebasket. Then he tells me to thank the Lord that I've been healed. What a nutcase! Who is he?" she spoke frantically.

"Says he's Jesus. Performs miracles," the doctor laughed.

"Sounds like a doctor," she answered dryly making no effort whatsoever to conceal her scorn for his much higher lever of remuneration.

They have returned to Danny's, and the crowds are enormous. They duck into Talk of the Town's back entrance and avoid all the media tumult going on out front.

The exterior of the bar is now completely draped in white lace with a white table and chairs in front of it, television cameras surrounding that.

It was to be a news conference with Jesus Christ. It would either be a ridiculous sham or the most earthshaking moment in the history of civilization.

"You know, if we had television the first time around for Jesus, imagine how much bigger he would have become," notes NBC correspondent Art Bogus, chatting away on camera with his co-anchor and NBC religion editor Edward O'Mally.

"Yes, Art, Jesus couldn't call on much of a media mix to get his message out in those early days. I dare to say, in his 33 years, he couldn't possibly have met as many people as one spot in a latenight talk show. Today, he'd be out of control. There'd just be no limit," adds O'Mally, smiling to the camera, sneaking that little wink he promised his wife, Suzzy, that he'd deliver.

It would be a good night for him tonight.

Harry is upstairs listening to an old Iron Butterfly disc.

Danny is talking away with the network's line pro-

ducer debating whether Harry can be seen in wide
shots with the news people. Danny insists that
Harry cannot be actively participating in the production of a television show and therefore must have
one camera constantly on him, never altering its
shot. The line producer explains that this is what
they would do anyway, but Danny demands that
they do it this way in spite of that. It's all very con-
fusing, but Danny is clearly in a position where he
must be dealt with and that's all he wants to prove
in the first place.

A cherry red Rolls Royce is led by three black
clothed Harley-Davidson types, the kind who used
to ravage innocent towns, not today's weekend
phonies, but these guys have been reformed. You
can see a certain serenity having taken hold where
all the hate used to be.

Everyone assumes that this must be the Messiah's
bunch.

The door is opened in front of Danny's. Out
comes two men in classic Church-white. Bishop
Flagg. Bishop Hutt.

"What have you gotten us into?" Hutt quietly
questions Flagg.

"He said we could meet him here, that's all I
know," answers Bishop Flagg.

"Have a seat Fathers. How do you like being
Priests, anyway, just curious," there goes Zeke.

They glare at him as he pulls out chairs at the long white table on the sidewalk, several thousand people staring, wondering what's going on, the two Bishops smiling softly, trying to look regal.

"What'll you have? On the house!" Zeke is so glad to be able to make such an offering.

"My friend, we are here on business. Where is this Harry Hamilton fellow and Mr. DeMarco?" asks Hutt.

"This spectacle is not appreciated," Flagg adds.

"Well, maybe a souvenir sweat band will get you in the spirit!" Zeke tries very hard to be a good host as he attempts to stretch the head band over Bishop Flagg's head gear.

The crowd notices movement in the upstairs room, the two curtains splitting slightly and two sets of eyes, one up high and one at knee level peering out. The lower eyes look delighted, the higher up ones look frightened.

"I am not going out there Danny," says Harry.

"Get your gown on, we're going. Just answer the questions in all honesty and I'll help you along," Danny assures him.

Harry slips the white muslin gown over his T-Shirt and jeans. Danny points to his Nike Air Jordans and gives them the thumb. Harry puts the sandals on and notes that they are fake Birkenstocks.

"I see the curtains in the main door stirring,"

notes Art Bogus and Ed O'Mally chimes in, "And so, it begins."

He continues, now reading from TelePrompTer "Two thousand years ago, a 33 year old carpenter's son gathered a following of believers, and was crucified for His efforts. To His death, this Jesus Christ denied his own divinity. The promise, that He will one day return and rise all of life to the heavens. This, then, possibly yes, possibly not, is that day. Art?"

Art does an equally nice job reading his lines.

"Ed, correct me if I'm incorrect here, but Jesus was noted as saying that to get to God you had to go through Him, isn't that true?"

Ed luckily scans the prompter before he reads it out loud. It says something about irregularity and hypertension pills, so he decides to ad-lib. "Art, we're talking about Jesus Christ here. I don't think He was involved in any managerial chain of command problems. This is the Son of God, for goodness sake. I don't think He applied himself to whether or not He had an exclusive relationship with His Holy Father, if that's what you're implying," he responds.

"Point, counterpoint, my friend," Art answers with a big All-American smirk on his face, which is luckily interrupted by the doors flipping open and Danny coming out in his red-on-red fashion statement along with the white-robed Harry. The crowd is completely silent.

"He's the Messiah like he's my left nut!" blurts Oscar the can man, who is often seen wandering downtown collecting empty aluminum cans, converting them to wine money to get him through the night on the County Administration Building underground parking lot floor.

"Shut the fuck up when you're in the company of the Lord!" snaps Pinkie, who is the first of the 36, now assigned to crowd control, to come to the defense of Harry.

"The Lord, my ass!" barks Oscar, who yanks a can from one of his bags and takes a contemptible bite out of it.

"Some people!" sighs Pinky as Oscar slumps to the ground, happy to behave himself now that he has something to chew on.

Danny introduces Harry to the two Bishops who don't know what to do so they both wave like little girls flirting with baseball players by the dugout.

Danny privately notes that JoAnne Conroy did a nice job with his makeup, but that she should cut back on the rouge a bit.

Danny takes the microphone as Harry sits to his left, the two Bishops to his right. Harry is flanked by both Father Pat and Father Mulroy, both dressed in the appropriate formal religious garb.

"Can you hear me?" Danny asks.

The crowd responds "Jesus Christ, Jesus Christ!" Danny notices that many of them have video cameras, and most of those are wearing undershirts and otherwise unkempt garb. He thinks to himself that this is the same crowd that congregates around the union tents at the local amusement park once a year. Jesus has somehow appealed primarily to people who gargle with beer.

Danny asks again, this time with a playful smile: "I said, can you hear me!!!???" and the crowd roars "Jesus Christ, Jesus Christ!!!"

"We must leave this place," Bishop Flagg whispers to Bishop Hutt. Bishop Hutt merely leers at Bishop Flagg for having brought him to this spectacle in the first place.

"Ladies and Gentlemen, men of the cloth, citizens of the world," Danny giggles to himself for the last reference, but he's not that far off. This is being beamed everywhere.

"No one at this table claims to be the Messiah. Indeed, everyone at this table would claim not to be. This is as it should be. But the fact is, and we are only here to introduce this man to the world – as a man with gifts, and nothing more – a great historic religious belief has spawned this day when 36 simple people on their own, coming from lives completely separated, came upon this man and knew in their hearts that he is, in fact, our savior returned to our civilization."

Danny continues as the two Bishops are slowly losing their natural skin tones, and the public is on their toes.

Oscar regains consciousness and Pinky brings him along by snapping an explosive bubble in his ear.

"Hey, who knows. God could be anyone these days," he informs her. "Maybe He's you!" and he laughs, "Maybe He's a she!!"

"My friends, we are joined here today by our nation's most esteemed representatives of the church, our local church leaders, and a very special group ladies and gentlemen, I ask you to stand and welcome – the 36."

Thousands of people already standing begin roaring "Thir-tee-six – thir-tee-six – " as Pinky and the others emerge from the crowd to stand at Danny's side.

Zero is tossing fake flowered necklaces to the crowd. Pinkie is shooting off bubble gum blasts ceaselessly, and Half-pint thinks he is having a PCP relapse.

"This is truly remarkable!" exclaims Art to the camera. Ed is as enthused. "Could this actually be? Has the day come??? By golly, it just might be!!!" exclaims the otherwise restrained scholar.

"I would like to begin by asking Bishop Flagg and

Bishop Hutt here if they could please begin this conference with their questions. And, of course, we understand that it is entirely in their role to be very cautious about this, and we appreciate their cooperation. Gentlemen," Danny tosses the ball and neither Bishop knows who should catch it.

So, Bishop Flagg takes the lead and says "Thank you. First, the Catholic Church believes in religious freedom and always has. When our Lord Jesus walked this planet, he attracted a following for His great wisdom and for the miracles that came forthwith. He never claimed to be the Son of God nor the Messiah. The Church would of course, not acknowledge anyone who did. So, what is the claim here?"

Danny quickly responds. "Very good question, Father. I now ask Harry Hamilton to answer. Mr. Hamilton, are you the Messiah? Are you Jesus Christ?"

Harry does not stand up. He taps the microphone and speaks easily. "No, that's what others have said. I make no such claim."

The entire crowd roars. Father Pat takes the microphone from Harry and says "My friends, many of you attend mass at my humble church, St. Matt's, and I ask you – who here has not seen evidence of the miracles performed by this humble man? Do we not want the Messiah to have returned? St. Matt's is a small church, but it is a church, and at St. Matt's we know one thing for certain – if there ever was a Messiah, he has returned."

He walks up to Harry and kneels, taking Harry's hand and kissing a knuckle.

"Hey back off!" whispers Harry. "I'm not that kind of Messiah," he giggles quietly.

Father Mulroy takes his turn.

"If we didn't have a Jesus Christ, we would have invented him. If we didn't have the Ten Commandments handed to us, we would have handed them to each other. These times require Jesus Christ. I welcome him."

The two Bishops are handed the microphone and Danny asks them if they have anything further to say.

Bishop Hutt has had it. He grabs the microphone and stands up. He notices that they are using that new wireless job and that it's transmitting to a nifty digital Nagra recorder that would go very nicely with his Ariflex BL that he uses to make vacation films.

"So, you're the Messiah, the one who was here before?" he asks Harry directly.

"I didn't say that. That's what they say."

"And this is your second coming, is it?"

"I don't know. They say so."

"Now, according to your teachings the first time around, this would pretty well mark the end of the world, so what's the status of that?"

"The world seems to be fine in my book," Harry responds as the audience laughs, rooting for the simple man to survive this tirade.

"So, why did you pick this time to return?"

"I'm sorry, but I wasn't part of the decision. I just got here. Ask mom," Harry is a bit tickled by the whole thing.

"Yes, and speaking of your mother, the way we've learned it, you caused her entire physical body to be assumed, to rise in to the heavens. Would you mind sharing with us how she's doing?"

Bishop Flagg does not care for either side of this public spectacle. He had always suspected that Bishop Hutt was simply a numbers guy that they had to dress in cloth, but this snarly side was too much to bear.

"I believe it is best for us to depart at this time," he says to Hutt.

"One last question, Mr. Hamilton, do you have any miracles planned for this time around?"

Danny takes the microphone from the completely confused Harry and says, "I'm glad you brought that up. The fact is that on July 5, the world will decide for itself," and Danny reveals the poster. "Ladies and gentlemen, we welcome you to the day the earth has awaited for two thousand years. Welcome to The Second Coming of Christ!"

The whole crowd goes nuts. Harry is led back into

the bar by Zeke. You are re-evaluating your entire being. The Bishops are a blur scampering toward their limos.

You notice that the door to the Rolls opens and Father Pat is sitting in the back seat. You can't read his lips but you know he's saying something to the bishops like, "I must talk to you."

The news people go on and on about modern civilization and what a shame it would be if we had everything but a Messiah during out lifetimes.

Frannie is near death and you all arrive at the hospital very late in the game.

"She has made no progress. Her vital signs are weakening," the surgeon reports while the nurse stands vigil.

"The clot shows no sign of regressing," the nurse looks to Harry who is utterly confused.

"I have healed hundreds of people, people who can't see, who can't walk. I can't believe she isn't responding, my own sister," Harry cries.

"It must take longer when its a relative," says Danny.

"This is taking things too far," Father Mulroy mumbles to Danny. "It's one thing to make a statement. This is a life."

"We've brought Harry to her bedside. How would you suggest we take this more seriously than that?!" Danny remarks disdainfully.

"Seriously, if we don't operate, I don't think she's likely to make it," cautions the surgeon. "We're on the verge of this being out of my hands."

"And just where is that verge, doctor?" Danny remarks. "Where is the line between a cure and a miracle?" he asks.

"When you deny the inevitability of death, that's when," the doctor answers quite seriously.

"And you, what do you think about that?" Danny says quietly.

"We can cure many things people once commonly died of. In that perspective, death proved inevitable only if you let it," answers the now introspective doctor. "Well, then, we're denying death once again," Danny comments.

"But with what cure? What new drug? What new procedure? You can't wish away her condition!" the doctor counters excitedly.

"With faith," Harry says solemnly. "Faith in what?" sneers the doctor, now returning to his skeptical, angry persona.

"Jesus," says Danny as he puts his arm around Harry. "Well, I'm tired of this argument. Let me just say one final thing gentlemen. He had better be Jesus, because in my estimation, that's becoming her only shot." The doctor walks away studying a chart.

Harry pulls Danny aside and they speak just out of earshot of Father Mulroy who is touching Frannie's cheek softly with his finger.

"Danny, if I'm not Jesus, then we're killing my sister."

"Harry, you've seen for yourself. We can't let her get operated on now, it'll destroy everything people believe in."

"Harry, you're Jesus Christ if you believe it. Do you believe it?" Father Mulroy steps in.

"I only know what I've seen. I've seen the impossible. What else could it be? I didn't sign up for this! I have no vested interest!!! I don't even have a job!!!!"

Harry is in a very excited state.

"You're Jesus," Danny jabs Harry's chin with his pointed finger. "I don't want to hear anything more about it." He turns away and almost collides with Father Pat who's walking in carrying his ant vial like it's a urine specimen.

He glances at Frannie, notices that the green lines on the monitor are sluggish.

"I have a concern," the quiet old Father says to Harry.

"What's that Father?" Harry can tell the man is disturbed.

"Harry, Isadora has not been healed. Surely, the Messiah can help Isadora walk again. The Bishops tell me this is a sign that you are a false Messiah. They say if I cannot read the signs, I cannot lead their Church."

Isadora is on her side wiggling her five good legs. "You again!" she mutters.

Harry looks to Father Pat and just to be a nice guy says "Sure, Father," and he takes the vial, carefully avoiding making eye contact with the Queen and says "Heal Isadora. Heal," and hands it back to Father Pat.

"If I can't heal an ant, I'd better find a new business, wouldn't you say Father!" Harry smiles.

Taking advantage of the lighter mood, despite Frannie still laying there motionless, Danny announces, "Frannie will be fine. Let's just give it a few more days. We must have faith or no one will. In a sense, Harry, the entire concept of faith is being tested here and now," Danny concludes, adding "She's important to me too, don't forget."

"I'm taking this to the courts," declares the surgeon.

"And who will they choose to judge me?" Harry counters.

"A psychiatrist would be my recommendation," the surgeon answers dryly.

"Why are you talking to me like that?" Harry steps up to the doctor.

"Are you a Christian?" Harry asks.

"I feel that I am," answers the doctor.

"Well, then, when the Messiah is to return, what exactly is it that you are expecting?" Harry continues.

"Certainly something more than a carnival act that finds a dying woman the cost of doing business," the surgeon says sadly.

This was the night that Harry escaped into the night. Only you know the details because you drove the car that took him to Beachwood, Ohio, where you believed more Jewish people lived than anywhere else in the state.

"The only people who would know for sure are Jews, Al. We've got to find some Jews," Harry had asked you.

"How would they know? They don't believe in Jesus!" you declared.

"I just want to find out if they'd believe I'm a Jew!" answered Harry. "So what?" you asked. "It's a starting place," said Harry and you drove to Corky & Lenny's deli, decorated like the Jewish version of a Chinese restaurant. You are checked out by all of the patrons, the old, slouchy fellow with thick black glasses sitting next to Harry at the counter studying both of you and then flatly commenting "Aren't you the guy they say is Jesus Christ?"

"Don't start," says Harry. "Can I have an egg roll?" he asks the waitress. "We don't sell egg rolls. How about an egg bagel?" she asks.

"Jesus was a Jew, you know," the guy continues. "You ain't a Jew, I hate to tell you," he adds.

"How can you know that?" Harry asks glumly.

"A Jew knows a Jew," the fellow says as he sashays away.

"How do you know?" Harry challenges him.

"Sing *Hava Na Gila*," the old guy instructs Harry.

"What's a *Hava Na Gila*?"

"If you were a Jew, you'd know."

"These are not conclusive tests!" you declare.

"He doesn't look like a Jew either," the guy adds. "Look at him. He's a Goy," he continues.

"Hey, you think you're Jesus Christ, that's fine

with me, but when the Messiah comes to this life, it's going to be heaven on earth. Let me ask you, have you seen any heaven lately?" the guy stops and his voice begins to feel a pain.

"I've seen some people who are happy," Harry says, sullenly. "I've seen some very sad people too," he adds. "My sister is dying," he tells the old man, and the man looks at you and looks at Harry and says "And where did Jesus come up with a sister, excuse me for asking?"

You and Harry leave the deli and head to downtown Cleveland where Harry wants a chance to get lost in the masses. You take him to an area called the Flats, a half run-down, half-renovated club type of area along the Cuyahoga River. You enter Peabody's Downunder, a big room that hasn't changed since Bruce Springsteen played there in his early days for free.

A rock n roll group is playing heavy metal Christian songs, and the lead singer catches sight of Harry.

He stops singing. The band stops playing. "I can't believe my eyes," the stringy-haired singer remarks. He looks very familiar to you.

"Pope," you say out loud. "Toledo!" the singer exclaims, now recognizing you from the early days at Danny's. "People, a person has walked in here....I don't know how to say it any other way than....I mean, this is Jesus, they say. What do you say!!!" he suddenly roars to the crowd, and they roar back "Jesus!!!" He strikes an outlandish chord on his beet red guitar.

"These are the people Harry. They know," you smile brightly.

Although most of the crowd is roaring drunk, their fascination with Harry is quite elating. "Jesus! Jesus!!! Jesus!!!!" they go on and on as they lift Harry in the air and start tossing him throughout the crowd as the band plays violent punk rock noise and Harry is flipping out like child.

Later, in the back of the Third District squad car, the policeman who pulled you both out of the place says quietly, "I'm going to pretend that none of this happened. Where's your car?"

"Officer, I'll take complete responsibility," says Harry.

"What's your name?" he asks you.

"What are you, a cop?" you laugh.

"What are you, a wise guy?" the policeman jokes.

"He's a wise man," Harry says serenely.

The policeman chalks you both up to what he'd expect from all the biological DNA stuff they're doing in the labs these days. "Don't come back to Cleveland if you know what's good for you," he says as you walk to your car.

"That's very kind," you say.

"I forgive you, officer," Harry says in his most

charming voice.

"Don't bother," the policeman groans.

"Fags," he spits as he gets in his car and calls the district to report that he's going to take a break at The Circus and check to make sure none of the strippers are showing too much of their own truth.

"I just don't know any more, Al," Harry confides in you. "What if I'm not Jesus. What if we're playing with Frannie's life!" he exclaims, very worried.

"Let the people decide," you advise. "You've seen how the real people respond," you add.

"Well that guy in the deli says I'm not Jesus. He seemed pretty certain," Harry reminds you.

"What does he know about Jesus? He's Jewish," you remind him.

"He'd be the one to know, wouldn't he?" Harry asks.

"Stop obsessing about this, Harry!" you advise. "If you're Jesus, super, we're all saved. If you're not, look at it this way: we need Jesus and you're not bad at it."

Another day. More people. "Let them cure themselves," you can hear Harry muttering. But this pair
is apparently different. They can walk and talk, see
and hear. Maybe they've cured themselves. Maybe
they have something uncurable.

"We just wanted to meet you."

"These are very special people, Harry. Meet Mr.
Spritz and Ms. Irons." Danny is so very gleeful.

Harry is popping a basketball up in the air with
his feet while he lies on the couch. "Good to meet
you."

"Well, Mr. DeMarco here tells me you have some
very special gifts. That you might in fact be the
Messiah. How do you feel about that?" Spritz asks
Harry.

"Well, Herb, if truth be told, I'd say the odds are
good that he's right, as outrageous as it seems," answers Harry, never taking his eyes off the bouncing
ball.

"And your show is something you believe in?" says
the ever skeptical Dolores Irons.

"Believe in?" Harry asks.

"I mean, you will be there, correct?" She is a
tough lady.

"He'll be there. With a whole bag of miracles,"
Danny promises.

"Now, exactly what will be the format?" asks
Herb.

"What do you mean, format?" Harry gives the gold-clad fellow an odd look. "I mean, do you go out there and tell stories or do you lead everyone in prayer? What do I know about Jesus? To me, I'd just want to see a few miracles."

"Oh, there'll be miracles," assures Danny.

"I once had my kid drag me to a Pink Floyd concert at Cleveland stadium. They had one point where pigs were flying in the air," Herb reminisces.

"Stuff like that?" he asks.

"Even bigger," smiles Danny.

"So, it's a go?" asks Herb.

"All indications are for a sellout, and we still have two days to go," answers Danny.

"I'd hold back a few miracles for a bigger city," advises Herb.

"Boss, boss! We're back," Zero calls through the thick wooden door as he bangs his feet against it, dust seeming to be jarred out of the grain.

The creaky door opens and a very solemn Father Pat looks toward Zero. "We need to talk. Gather them all in the chapel," he instructs the concerned man. Zero looks on the other side of the Father's desk and sees two far more distinguished men of the cloth. He's seen Bishop Hutt's picture somewhere, and he can tell that Bishop Flagg is a big gun as well. He can tell that both of them are feeling hopeful, for some odd reason.

"We're all here," Zero assures him. "Don't have much time though, we're all getting ready for the show," he says enthusiastically.

"Oh, yes. And what is your role?" asks the tired Father.

"Hospitality!" gloats Zero. Pinky reveals that she's been at his side all along. "Ushers," she adds. "And we can keep the tips."

"Meet us in the chapel," Bishop Hutt tells them, and they leave the Father with his high level visitors.

"You'd think he'd be more excited," comments Zero. "I don't think he was really ready for the Messiah, if you want to know the cold truth," notes Pinky. "I don't know if anyone really is," she says under her breath as they join the rest of their flock and nervously await Father Pat.

The Father and the Bishops saunter to the chapel. Father Pat's knees crack with every step up to the pulpit.

"You've received the sign, now share it," Bishop Hutt instructs the weakened Father Pat.

"My friends, in the name of the Father, the Son, and the Holy Ghost, Amen." He lifts his hands feebly to his side. The Bishops lift their hands to their sides slowly like penguins.

"There has been a passing on," the Father mutters.

"Who kicked the bucket?" Half-Pint pops up like the "No Sale" flag on an old cash register.

"The charade has ended," Bishop Flagg ignores the question.

"The evidence is undeniable," Father Pat adds sorrowfully.

It's not that Danny isn't feeling the tension as he listens to the doctor on the telephone. "Mr. De-Marco, the only thing keeping her alive right now is life support. On her own, she wouldn't last the evening," the surgeon reports.

Danny is aware that he's cutting it real close, but the timing is near perfect. The show is at 8pm and they can be back at the hospital easily by 11.

"We'll be there tonight. If she hasn't made a turn, we'll give our permission," Danny answers.

"It may be too late," warns the doctor.

"Doctor, if there was ever a night when a miracle could happen, this is it, trust me. There's going to be more miracles than we know what to do with," Danny promises.

The day of the Second Coming has arrived with
an onslaught of lawyers.

Bishop Hutt is on the phone with the gentleman
from the Vatican. Bishop Flagg is pretending none
of this is happening.

"They are readying to ship their merchandise
everywhere you go," Hutt says politely to the Pontiff.

"There is no legal recourse?" he asks.

"We're trying, but no one owns the rights to the
Second Coming or in fact, to Jesus Christ, although
we are claiming ownership by usage."

"How is this effecting our distribution?"

The fact was that given a choice, your grand-
mother likes to collect things with the official licensed Pope image on them, but the real thing
these days is a genuine "Second Coming" garment.

"You must close this thing down and destroy this
merchandise!" pleads the attorney for the Church to
the bailiff of Judge Surcumfry over at Toledo Munic-
ipal Court. "They are blaspheming the Church!"

"It's still a free world, isn't it sir?" remarks the
young law student working for her father the judge
that summer.

"They are capitalizing on images created by the
Church, our proprietary property!" he continues.

"You are claiming to own the image of Jesus
Christ?" she asks.

"This man is an impostor. The entire event is a fraud!!!"

"Then why has not a single ticket holder claimed so?" she continues.

Bishop Flagg rises from his seat and walks to the lawyer's side.

"With all due respect, if the court would inspect the event's grounds, she might see that this is not true," he suggests.

"He is not Jesus Christ!!!!" the attorney beseeches her.

"We have proof," Bishop Flagg announces.

"And what would that be?" she asks.

The Bishops and the attorney had previously decided that this particular proof might stretch the court's vision a bit beyond the limit. They'd save it for a more propitious moment.

"The proof is that his healing powers are fraudulent. He could not be Jesus Christ," the Bishop answers softly.

"Let me ask, did the man say he was Jesus?" she questions with quiet confidence.

"Everyone around him acts like he is, and that's what is driving thousands to come see him," bellows the attorney.

"For hundreds of dollars each in some cases," adds the Bishop.

"We're just asking for a cease and desist. We really

should be demanding their arrest," the attorney continues.

"Well, now, did they arrest those who said the same thing two thousand years ago?" she asks.

"No, but they crucified him!" the attorney attacks.

"Thankfully, we're a bit more civilized today. Why don't we just let the public make up its own mind," she concludes.

"Then we demand equal access to this public property."

"Granted!" Danny DeMarco bursts in to the chambers and pokes his chin right in to the belly of the rotund attorney.

"Bring your Bishops and your dukes and the Crusaders and all your friends and neighbors and we'll be glad to welcome you," Danny offers. "Here's some tickets. Come see for yourself," he smiles.

"Mr. DeMarco, I am a lawyer. I don't care about religion one bit. What I'm telling you is that you are defrauding the public and defaming the church." To the young bailiff he says "And young lady, I am entitled to an immediate judgment regarding my request for an injunction to shut this thing down, and I caution you to adhere to your duties to this court."

"I'll talk to Dad about it."

"Well get to it!"

"He's in Argentina."

"What's he doing in Argentina???"

"Some last minute private consulting for a very wealthy individual there."

She and Danny who have never really met, exchange a knowing giggle and they both understand that the public doesn't place high criteria on the honesty of things that entertain them.

"You know, for a group that has been fretting about the Messiah for such a long time, it sure is odd that you immediately jump to the defensive when there's a chance he might actually have done what you said he would," Danny says.

"Oh, and what would that be?" asks the Bishop.

"Returned," says Danny.

"That's quite doubtful under the circumstances," the Bishop answers dryly.

Danny steps right in front of the Bishop and answers.

"You know, from moment one, I don't believe that you people ever even considered the possibility that Jesus had returned. Now, why would that be?" he asks.

"He was clearly a fraud," the Bishop answers.

"Oh, is that so? And you knew this right from the get-go?" Danny asks.

"Absolutely. From the highest authority," answers Bishop Flagg authoritatively.

"Then maybe you are more surprised at the possibility of Jesus returning than you should be, considering that this is what you've been preaching since he left," Danny argues.

"We're expecting that there will be more to him than there is of your Harry," answers the Bishop.

"And it wouldn't be too good for business either, now would it?" smiles Danny.

The bailiff smiles back at Danny. The Bishop is aghast. The lawyer puts his arm around the Bishop and walks him out as the bailiff calls to them.

The entrance paths to the Mud Hen's stadium
are clogged with all sorts of people. Families. Guys
with tattoos. Women with tattoos. Kids who are excited for the day when they'll have tattoos. The fathers are not wearing suits and ties like you'd see at
a miracle tent. The mothers are not wearing Easter
bonnets. Everyone is dressed for mud wrestling or
tractor pulling or some sort of gritty spectacle like
that.

An hour before curtain and even you have back-
stage jitters. You're surrounded by cables running
every which way, all flowing like big snakes to a huge
panel of switches behind the gold lame curtain at
the left side of the stage.

Darryl is wearing his entire tool chest around his
waist and seems to be entirely in control of the tech-
nicalities.

The stage has one huge protruding pulpit rising
like the spine of a swan high in to the air. There is
room for just one person. The one person who
28,000 people have paid an average of $100 a ticket
to see. And that's at box office prices. Scalpers have
been in the $500 territory. You know that for a fact,
because Danny's had you and Zeke sell quite a number for the price on the street.

Where's Harry?

You look way up high to Harry who is presently
being fitted in his white satin cape over his black

stretchy body suit. He looks more like a wrestler than a Messiah, but you can't see that it matters. At least he looks like the good guy.

His beard has grown nicely. His hair is properly shaggy. Harry looks over to you with that silent bleating expression that says, "This is not good, Al." And you return the gaze and he knows that you are sympathetic.

Danny is on the stage and calls you over.

"I want you to witness this and never forget it," says Danny with his fatherly arm around you. Whenever Danny puts his arm around anyone, he ends up patting their butt because that's as high as he reaches, but he means no molestation, of the body anyway.

"This is what man can do when he has faith," Danny mutters proudly.

You look out on the field and see a coffin sitting elegantly on huge roman columns. You see a small lake filled with fish. This you want to see more closely.

There's a bed of hay where loaves of bread sit on wooden planks. An entire Bible of religious relics is spread throughout the field.

Father Mulroy is rubbing Harry's back. "This isn't a sham is it father?" Harry asks and Father Mulroy answers as always, "All that we need we invent. When you walk outside ask yourself, what do they need."

"What do they need, Father?" Harry asks.

"Apparently you."

"Check out the crowds, will you Al?" Danny asks you. You take a walk down the concrete walkway and go outside the stadium where you see Pinky with a scowl on her mouth trying to direct traffic away from the entrance and toward the ticket booths.

"Refunds right this way," she exclaims. "All windows are open for refunds."

You walk to your left and you see Half-Pint in a pirate uniform slashing his sword in the way of the entrance, aiming people to the same ticket windows.

"He ain't Jesus!" he tells a young father dragging his two little kids who are skidding on their dress shoes toward the gate.

"Hey, what are you a troublemaker?" he accosts Half-Pint.

"He ain't Jesus, I'm doing you a favor!" the little pirate repeats.

"Well you don't have to say so in front of the kids!" the father retorts and drags his kids onward.

You walk further and there's Zero doing the same.

"Refunds at the ticket windows folks. Refunds to the left," he tries to direct traffic. He looks very disappointed, genuinely hurt as an older woman comes up to him.

"What's going on here?" she asks angrily.

"We found out that he's not who they say he is, ma'am," answers Zero.

"Well, neither is Santa Claus but we don't sit here on Christmas Eve screeching it!" she snaps.

"Madam, do you realize that you have been made a fool of?" a voice comes from behind. It's Bishop Hutt walking along aside Bishop Flagg. Father Pat tries to keep up.

"Says who?" the old, feisty woman shrieks.

"Says God," Bishop Flagg proclaims.

"And what army?" she retaliates.

A small crowd has surrounded them as Zero continues offering them the quickest route to a refund.

"All thirty six of The 36 say so," Bishop Hutt explains. "They have denounced him," concludes Bishop Flagg.

"It was a sign from God," mutters Father Pat.

You would do something about this except you can't help but notice that the ticket windows for the sold out event have no customers. No one wants a refund. The stadium is filling.

You return to the control area and watch all the crew carrying cables, lifting this, moving that. No one seems to be telling anyone what to do. You imagine that they communicate through some kind of vibration as they pass by each other, like in the ant farms.

"Let's go," Danny sticks his head in and notes on

his clipboard that we followed yet another of his own procedures.

Harry and Father Mulroy begin the long walk toward the stage. From way behind, Father Pat struggles to catch up.

The phone rings behind them. You answer.

"She's almost gone," says the voice from the hospital.

"If we don't get permission within moments, she will die."

"He's not here. He's going to do his miracles now."

"He had better not waste any."

The phone goes silent.

Chapter Fifty One

Harry is high in the air over the stage by himself, hidden by the enormous white fabric column which will lift up as he slowly descends to the stage. He's standing on a small metal lift. It has a matching platform above him so he can grab hold of something if it gets too shaky.

The lights go out. Harry begins his descent, his hair and robe flowing in the winds caused by the enormous turbines coming out of everywhere.

"Harry! Listen to me!!!!" the voice is coming from above.

"Hello?" Harry looks up and sees nothing but the bottom of the steel platform.

"Harry, you aren't Jesus," the voice bellows. "You are not the Messiah. You're just Harry."

It's Father Pat. He is shaking as he climbs down from the platform and ends up standing next to Harry as they both continue descending toward the bright light where they'll land on stage.

They hear Danny's loud voice over the powerful sound system.

"Ladies and gentlemen, the most awaited moment in the history of civilization is upon us."

But that moment is being ignored by Father Pat and Harry.

"All of these kind of miracles are manmade, Harry," Father Pat explains as he takes Harry's hand, tears open the gold lame fabric backdrop to reveal

Darryl standing there, leather gaffer gloves around his hands, big levers everywhere ready to be pulled.

"I know that these miracles are not mine, Father, but that's showbiz. But you've seen what I've been able to do," Harry explains.

"I gave it the benefit of doubt too, until this happened, a passing on," and Father Pat reaches in his pocket and presents the medicine vial to Harry.

The Queen is dead. Harry can see in her wide open eyes that her last though was the humiliation of having died from a bum leg."

"I couldn't heal an ant," Harry drops his head in sorrow.

"You could never hurt one either," reminds the Priest.

"But all those others..."

"Your sister is not healing either."

They land on the platform and the fabric column rises as the audience roars.

"Pull them," Father Pat demands to Darryl.

Danny can see what's going on and gets very nervous.

"Ladies and Gentlemen – one moment for..."

"Pull them Darryl. Jesus says so," Harry orders.

"In just one moment –" Danny continues as he casts a watchful eye behind the scenes.

"She won't last the hour and Harry must know the truth if we're going to have any real miracles tonight."

And never again in the history of man and woman would there ever be such a preponderance of miracles performed at one place in one time. A dozen loaves of bread turn in to thousands, all flipping from concealed containment areas, floating through air, helium powered. A tiny stream of water becomes a river of red. And Lazurus rises once again, the great coffin ascending high in to space and in to the clouds.

You feel quite a rumbling yourself, and that little Plexiglas platform you've been standing on to watch the fish suddenly slings across the lake, stops suddenly and pitches you into the miracle pool.

A little Lake Erie perch throttles over to you and explains in frothy bubbles and alternating cheek inflations that when you are alone, you can drown in your own element.

You think to yourself, "Survival is not an individual endeavor." Now is the time to revel in the unity of life, a power so strong and inevitable, even failure can't detract from its truth.

You have the keys to the car, and the hospital is awaiting.

The Queen has died, but Frannie doesn't have to.

"Daddy, is that all there is? It only lasted five minutes," cries a little girl held tight by her father walking through the congested traffic outside the stadium.

"But it was sensational. It was like nothing I've seen since the war," he proudly declares to his little love bucket.

You note that everyone else seems pretty satisfied as well and it occurs to you that reality can never live up to the fantasies we've learned to bring to life. No wonder so many of our capabilities are aimed at creating virtual this and virtual that. Nothing is as grand as illusion.

"Start the surgery!" Danny screams as he blasts through the sliding hospital doors. "You have my permission."

"It's a little late for miracles." The nurse makes no effort to contain her contempt as you, Danny, Harry and the two Fathers rush in to Frannie's room. All of The 36 are gathered outside the room. Pinkie and Zero are standing on the backs of Half-Pint and Dayglo, peering through the window.

"It's a funny life," Pinky whispers to Zero.

"I'm sorry we had to go against you, Harry, but I guess we picked he wrong guy," Zero apologizes to Harry as the rest of them gesture the same sentiments.

"We didn't mean any harm," adds Pinky.

Very little of Frannie is visible. Her head is covered with an oxygen mask. Tubes are going in and out of her every which way. You don't see much evidence of breathing, and even though you can't read any of the displays on the computers, it's pretty clear that there isn't much life left to read about.

"She isn't going to make it," the nurse reports sadly.

"Her signs are almost undetectable. She hasn't moved a centimeter since yesterday. You can hardly call her alive," the nurse bitterly concludes.

The gurney is pushed toward her bed, a nurse and surgeon ready to take her. The first nurse thrusts a signature page at Danny, she practically stabs him with the pen and waits for his signature on the surgical release.

"She's going to make it," says Harry decisively as he gets on his knees and reaches for Frannie's lifeless arm and clutches it to his face.

"Cut it, Harry!" Danny's tears are smearing the ink as he begins signing his name.

"Oh, if it isn't the Lord our God," snarls the surgeon who is watching carefully over what he knows to be a hopeless situation.

"And if it isn't the Lord our doctor," Harry sneers back as he gets on his knees, shuts out the world outside of him and the sister he loves.

"Oh, Lord our God, hallowed be His name. Lord Jesus, a terrible thing has been done in Your name and I offer myself to You in case somehow You've confused the innocent with the guilty. Believe me, Lord, that my sister here would never do a thing against another, and I admit that I went astray and allowed this charade to go on, and I know that the way to hurt me the most would be to hurt my sister here, but I offer You my eternity for any punishment You see fit if only You let Frannie have her nice life. I know she has always devoted herself to You. That's what we were taught. And me and Danny and Al here, we don't deserve one bit of Your forgiveness, just don't punish the wrong person,

Jesus."

Danny kneels beside Harry. He has never knelt in his lifetime. He has never prayed.

"I can only say this, that, uh, well, I never knew what faith was until I gave my faith to the wrong thing and saw how easy it was to just play with it. Frannie here is the only person in the entire world that I love. And You should not forgive me. I don't ask for that. I only know one thing, Jesus. I coulda made all Your miracles happen once again and nobody woulda known the difference. I coulda healed a thousand blind people and no one would doubt it."

He continues as everyone is now on their knees praying at her bedside, the hospital staff taken by the scene, yet anxious to take their patient away.

"But I could never have saved one real person, Lord, we never could have responded to one real prayer.

I may be the worst person who's ever asked You for anything, but I can promise You this, Jesus. You've never heard a more real prayer. Save her and take me. Do what You will with me, just don't let life have no meaning at all. Don't let a decent person just go like that." Danny has real tears in his eyes and his knees give way as he falls to the bed, his weeping eyes moistening Frannie's fingers.

"Al, talk to Him, please, help me say the right things," Danny begs you.

You struggle through a lifetime of prayer and can't reach inside for the right words. You want to open your Bible randomly and hope for divine intervention to provide the perfect plea, but failing that, you close your eyes and gently touch Frannie's hand.

And then you remember from your Bible: "As by one man's disobedience many were made sinners, so by the obedience of one shall many be made righteous." It's all you have.

Frannie stirs.

It's all you need.

Frannie's eyes quiver.

"You'll have to leave!" the nurse pulls the emergency cord and you are almost knocked over by the rush of eager men and women in white masks.

"Thank you Lord." Danny is being yanked away from the bed but he reaches down and kisses Frannie on her cheek. Her dry lips part and her eyes struggle to open. Danny says "You don't have to say a thing, Frannie. It's enough that you're alive."

But the struggle continues. Her mouth quivers. She whispers feebly in Danny's ear: "I think Saturn Split."

Danny answers with a smile moistened by tears "Well, thank God Jesus didn't."

"And I'm not referring to you," he growls to Harry.

You can't help but notice the hint of a smile in Frannie's closed eyes.

You and Harry are pushed out the door by the onslaught of medical personnel. You look behind at Frannie and there is no mistaking the hint of a weak smile on her face. And in that moment, you all share the truth, that love is the real miracle of life.

Zero and friends are intoxicated by the miracle. "He must be Jesus!" exclaims Zero.

"Who?" Harry glares as you squish him against the door jamb.

"Someone!" answers Pinky. Philosophy and spiritualism seem to have united, and every one finds the moment quite giggly in a relieving way.

"Could we re-negotiate the part about taking me?" Danny looks to the ceiling as you drag him out of the room.

"Maybe that was a little severe. I wasn't thinking clearly!!!" he continues negotiating with some power which he is no longer embarassed to believe in.

Chapter Fifty Three

The next night, Danny asks if you'll drive him back out to that Turnpike exit, and he seems very sad and pessimistic as you ride him in silence to the strange destination.

You leave him and drive to an area fast food place, and behind in the mirror you see that faint yellow light illuminating his round features, life looking like it has very little interest in itself.

"Is Mary Chu there please? This is Danny De-Marco," Danny asks and expecting the same rude reply as before hears, "You wait one minute."

He waits and a very young girl takes the receiver and says: "Mr. DeMarco?"

"Yes."

"Mary Chu has not been here for a very long time.

"I would like very much to see her."

"Where are you?" the surprisingly pleasant voice asks.

He explains the location and she asks for the phone number. He gives it to her and she asks him to wait. He strolls over toward the rental cottages and is agonized over the truth that no spectacle of any size can relieve the need for a private embrace with someone you can share a laugh or a tear with. In this thought, Danny finds hope.

Hours go by and he calls again.

"I was calling about Mary Chu," he says.

"No Mary Chu here," the impatient voice answers.

"But I was told you might find her..."

"She find you," the voice promises and hangs up.

Danny sifts through his memory while leaning against the discolored glass. He remembers how proud he had been of his restraint, his confidence that in his heart, he is a decent man. He feels empty and full at the same time.

His eyes are closed in frustration. "I need to see her just once again," he whispers to the insects fluttering around the dim yellow light.

A voice comes from outside the door of the telephone booth.

"Well, first you must open your eyes."

Her beautiful hair is flowing in the wind.

"I don't know what to say." Danny brings her in to the booth, lets the receiver fall and hugs her like a baby clutching his teddy bear.

"This time, let our natures be in control," she whispers. "Nature is truth. Our instincts are God," she clutches him and leads him down the hill where they fall to the soft grass and let their feelings unite.

They would never see each other again. They would never need to. Danny had the one truth he prayed to know. He has a real heart. Someone can have deep feelings toward him. He can toy with the rest of the world. There is nothing wrong with being unreal when you're dealing with the unreal, as long as you have a heart that can feel real love.

"It's a funny world," he says as they part.

"Go outside and play in it," she kisses him softly and disappears.

Epilogue

"It's over," said the hushed voice of Bishop Hutt as he carefully guarded his relief while talking on the phone to the small voice at the Vatican.

"Are you sure?" asked the quiet man.

"No one will ever try that again," assured Bishop Hutt as he drew another card in his Blackjack game on the new pocket-sized multi-media computer.

"Well, we do hope it happens once, don't we, Bishop Hutt?" the voice suggested with a hint of a smile.

"In due time," concluded the Bishop as he drew on a sixteen against the computer's exposed Queen, and broke with a ten. Just for laughs, he drew again, another picture card for a total of thirty six, at which time he turned the darned thing off.

Danny is in the back room where he spends most of his time these days.

"So, how's it going?" you ask.

"It's going very nicely," he utters without smiling.

"That sounds nice. What are you making?"

"I'm making impressionistic personal items," he snarls.

"What d'ya mean?" you ask, genuinely curious.

"Intimate things. Condoms. Big condoms with nature scenes on them. I'm working with one I call Old Faithful. The geyser," he smiles just a bit.

"That's very inventive. You might have something there," you laugh.

"I'm doing another of that place with the President's heads on it, what's that place?" it's on the tip of his tongue. "Rushmore. Mount Rushmore. Get it?" He's elated that his memory still functions.

"Well, Danny, I'm glad that Frannie is doing much better now. The doctors say it really was a miracle," you change the subject.

"It just goes to show the value of prayer. And the faith in the big man almighty," he glances up to make sure God can hear him.

"Harry's still not working, but he was on Bryant Gumbel this morning," you update Danny.

"What's he trying to pass himself off as these days, John Lennon?" Danny quips.

"Harry?" you ask?

"No, Gumbel!" Danny finally laughs.

"They're all Jesus. They're all God. Come on, if Walt Disney wasn't a God, who is? And Dustin Hoffman!!! He's a Messiah! Minimum!!! But do you see any of them with the court on their tails? I don't see them!" Here he goes again.

"I don't see them either Danny" you try to pacify him.

Danny was in jail for a mere night, but that was enough time for him to get all the interested parties together and work things out. Herb Spritz got all of his money back. He and Dolores are winging their way back to Argentina where he intends on providing her the life of her dreams, replete with some new ideas he has related to crushed bananas and stilleto heels.

Thankfully, almost miraculously, the judge found it appropriate to close the matter at that point. The show produced a ton of profit, so Danny was able to almost pay his entire attorney bill.

"I didn't see Bob Hope in the can. Or Jerry Lewis. Or that damn grinning Paul McCartney or Elton John! You don't see any of them in the can, but every one of them has waltzed around as a God," Danny continues.

"I don't believe any of them have claimed to be God, Danny," you gently suggest.

"Yeah, but what's that matter? Actions. Words. They're all the same. I think Harry was the only one on earth who literally denied being Jesus! And I end up in jail!!! You make sense out of it."

You know that it's best to just let him wear it out.

"And I want you to know one more thing!" Danny grips your attention.

"Whatever you say, Danny, you're the boss," you truly feel for the man.

"That's what I want to say," Danny softens and smiles a little smile at you. The real smile he so seldom reveals.

"You're the boss now," he puts his hand out for you to shake.

"Take over the management of the place for me and make it work," he instructs you, and you shake his hand vigorously.

"Just let me have this area to do my work. And a nightly count, of course," he smiles. "You'll get your cut," he adds.

You saunter through the bar and give a pleasant smile to Zeke who figures life goes on and he's ready for whatever comes. Zero and Pinky are setting up the new kitchen in the space where the embroidery equipment used to be. Along with the other veterans of the Second Coming, they intend on working to generate income for Father Pat's new homeless shelter, which continues to reside in St. Matt's. A little sign hangs over the kitchen area which says "For Christ's Sake."

"We don't hold any grudges, boss," said Zero when they worked out the plan with Danny. "We don't work for anyone, and we don't work against anyone," he added. "We just always do what we think is right," said Pinky.

"Got to hand it to you, though, Boss," Zero said. "You gave the people what they wanted."

"What's that, Zero?" Danny asked glumly.

"Something to look forward to," Zero quickly answered.

Father Mulroy is hanging out smoking a pipe, every now and then giggling out loud, enjoying the knowledge that he was right all along. Still, no calls from the Vatican asking him to come back, and you're sure he'd be entertained by the chance to turn them down.

You're looking forward to Frannie coming home. She'll have a special place here.

You walk up to the horse's head and close its eyes for good. You put an old Zorro blindfold on him just in case he tries to sneak a look. You have some ideas of your own and this is a great launching pad for quirky concoctions.

You're thinking that maybe Danny is really just like all of us. We all reveal good hearts, given the right time and place. Nothing else really separates us.

The End Is Not Yet.

Jesus
Matt 24:6

About the Author

Alan Glazen is a leading advertising writer, director and composer. He has received over 50 industry awards. His commercial production company, Glazen Creative Group, creates and produces memorable films, videos, radio, music and print material for commerce and entertainment. Mr. Glazen wrote "The Trial of Anna Hahn," a stage play produced in Cleveland, Ohio. He is currently writing a stage play for release in Spring , 1995.

Correspondence may be directed to:
Glazen Creative Group
812 Huron, Suite 500
Cleveland, Ohio 44115
(216) 241-7200